THE
OPENING

a novel by Ron Savarese

Home
Planet
Publishing

The Opening

THE OPENING
A Novel

Published in the USA by Home Planet Publishing

ISBN: 0615460763

ISBN-13: 978-0615460765

Book design and layout by Benjie Nelson

Printed in the United States of America

This is a Home Planet Publishing Book

for Dougie

When I die, I will soar with the angels,
And when I die to the angels,
What I shall become,
You cannot imagine.

Rumi

THE OPENING

WITH THE ANGELS

The day before the child departed I sat with him under a willow tree near the banks of the crystal waterfall. His feet grazed the blanket as he positioned himself cross-legged next to me.

It's time for our story now, I said. It's about a man who has to make a difficult choice and a little child like you who goes on a journey. Are you ready?

He rocked back and forth ever so slightly with his arms wrapped around his knees. He placed his hands behind him on the blanket and leaned back.

I Am, he said.

THE APPOINTMENT

My appointment with death was less than a month away.

I had no idea at the time. I started the day with my usual routine. I woke up early, sat on the bed, and looked out the window. I shuffled down the hall, drank a cup of coffee, and took a shower. I got dressed, kissed my wife good-bye, and went to the office—just another ordinary day. Or so I thought.

I didn't actually schedule the appointment. You could say I brought it upon myself. But that might be overstating things just a bit. So let's just say it was an accident and leave it at that for now.

I thought my appointment with death would come much later in my life. I don't know why. I guess I liked to imagine I would die in my own bed, at a ripe old age with my family around me. Or better yet, pass away peacefully in my sleep.

Nothing can really prepare you for your final moments. You just live and breathe and try to be happy. And when your number gets pulled, it's your time. Well, that's what I thought. But it didn't quite work out that way for me.

Oh, I know what you might be thinking. You're going to have some time to prepare. You're going to have some idea your time is approaching. You might. But I didn't. I had no idea. Not even a hint.

Now I know it was the little decisions I made along the way that lead me to my destiny. Or away from it. I didn't believe that then. But I believe it now.

I don't know if it was my destiny to have a conversation with my wife Jessica on that drizzly, November night. And I don't know if it was that conversation that brought me to the appointment. But there's no doubt in my mind—after the conversation, the appointment was set.

In retrospect, I guess there were signs. I see that now. Perhaps if I had been more tuned in I would have noticed. God knows I'd been taught.

Some say death is a big sleep. A big dream. I wonder. I wonder which is the bigger sleep or the bigger dream. Life or death?

It didn't matter.

My appointment had already been penciled in.

THE CONVERSATION

It was cold that November evening and I had just driven home through the rain from a meeting with one of my key financial advisors. He confirmed what I already knew, and what I didn't want to know. Things did not look good. I'd hit a cold streak. I had invested far too much of my money in technology and telecom stocks and several internet ventures that were on the verge of bankruptcy.

Stock prices had become stretched to ridiculous proportions. A severe correction was underway. It was a year ago when I said to my advisor, "I think we should sell some of those tech stocks—cut back on some of our positions. Those companies don't have the earnings to justify the prices."

"It's not about the earnings," he said. "It's about clicks and e-commerce. We're in a new economy now. The Internet is going to change everything. I think we should add to our positions on any pullbacks."

Fortunately, I didn't add to my positions. But I didn't cut back on them either. Now I was paying the price. And if the market correction wasn't bad enough, my real estate holdings were all leveraged to the hilt, and the debt which I had been trying to refinance for the past several months was strangling my cash flow.

On the home front, my wife Jessica had been diagnosed with cancer less than a year before. She had recently completed chemotherapy treatments. The doctors said the treatments had done what they had hoped—they thought they caught it early enough—but we all knew her future was uncertain. There were no guarantees. Our marriage, which was rocky before her illness, had recently become even more strained.

To top it all off, my relationship with my three children, Caryn and John—both away at college—and Thomas, a junior in high school, had deteriorated to the point where we seemed to speak only out of necessity. Just a few years ago, they had looked to me as a role model, a loving father, someone they could come to for guidance and support. But now as I battled the demons of mid-life, financial losses, and a growing dependence on alcohol, the chasm between us had widened to uncomfortable proportions.

It was my fault I guess, I was working too much; traveling and drinking and staying out late trying to get deals done.

Yeah, things didn't look good. Yet in spite of my souring relationships, and compulsions, and financial woes, I still had enough money to live "the good life." I was fairly well set. I didn't need to worry about money. Too much. There were a couple of problems, though. One problem: my life wasn't very "good" anymore. It was a struggle just to get up in the morning, make it through a day, and get back in bed at night.

So that night I settled into my typical after-work routine. I sat on the back porch with a bottle of bourbon at my side. I stared out at the ocean through the branches of a few tall palms and watched a half moon rise between the clouds of a starless gray night. As I contemplated my situation, I sipped my fourth glass of straight bourbon over ice, something I'd done far too often both before and after dinner the past year.

With each sip, I watched Jessica through the back door window as she put the last of the dishes into the dishwasher. In spite of her condition, she carried on with remarkable strength. She continued her P.R. career and even found the energy to work with her charities. I admired that about her. Where did her strength come from? If I were in her shoes, I wouldn't be able to do it. She's a hell of a lot stronger than me, I thought. And she has a big heart.

Oh sure, don't get me wrong. I did my part. I could throw the money in, make an appearance at a cocktail party or black-tie, make a speech, and get the credit. But Jesse put in the time and the touch. And that's what really matters. Once I used to care about the sort of things Jessica cared about, but things had changed. I'd become self-centered, Jesse said. I didn't necessarily think that was true. But if it was, what the hell did she want me to do about it? That "self-centeredness" had provided well for our family.

I knew Jessica was more worried about me than she was about herself. She was just made that way I guess. She told me she thought my mood swings had gotten worse lately and I was drinking too much. It was time for me to consider professional help, she said. So I did. She was a worrier. That's probably why she had the cancer and I had the depression.

Battles seemed to be burning like wild fires everywhere in my world that November. I battled everything. I guess I just liked a good fight. I liked the competition. Truth is I enjoyed the battles. Besides, if you're going to get ahead in this world, you've got to fight for every dollar. And don't let anybody tell you any different. That's just the way it is.

So I battled with attorneys over contracts and clauses. I battled with bankers over loan repayments and interest rates and where to price deals. I battled with my partners over percentages of ownership and dominion over our clientele. I battled with my children over the choices they made with their lives. It seemed like I was battling everybody and everything, including myself.

It's true. One part of me liked a good fight, but another part of me had grown tired of negotiating deals with men in navy blue suits and button-down shirts. I had hit the wall. Hard. What had happened to my ambition? My motivation? What had happened to my drive? I was tired of the long hours in corporate boardrooms and late night dinners and drinks. I wanted freedom. I wanted to live my life the way I wanted to live it. I wanted to feel passionate about something again. I wanted meaning. I wanted peace.

And that was the other problem: I didn't even know what I was passionate about anymore or how I wanted to live. It seemed the only thing that had any meaning to me was making money and showing my superiority. It seemed like I was always judging, always comparing myself to the other guys. It seemed as if somewhere along the road to becoming a master of success, I'd lost my way.

Something inside of me had changed, but my life remained the same. Something had shifted, yet I was stuck in a rut of my own making. What happened to me? When did this change occur? And where was I when it happened? These were the questions I asked myself that night, and yet, no answers came. So I stifled myself, and languished away on bourbon, or anything else that numbed the emptiness and hid the truth and feelings I didn't want to confront. And as the fire in my belly smoldered into burned-out ashes of a half-lived life, I felt as though I was losing my grip.

I was depressed. No doubt about it. But no one had a clue about my depression except Jessica. My doctor had prescribed some anti-anxiety and anti-depression medication, but that didn't seem to do much good. And besides, the meds gave me pounding headaches. So it was back to the old stand-by for me: bourbon, before and after dinner.

It was just getting windy enough that I was thinking should I fill my bourbon glass again or head inside to bed, when Jessica opened the door and stepped out onto the porch. She stood just behind me, her hand resting lightly on my shoulder. "What is it, Jesse?" I asked.

"Are you okay? I'm worried about you," she said. She snuggled in behind me and kissed my cheek. "You've been sitting out here a long time. What are you thinking about?"

I used to share all my thoughts with Jessica. We were so close then we seemed to be one person. But lately that question just irritated me. I didn't answer.

She patted my chest then wrapped her arms around me. "It's going to be okay. Things are never as bad as they seem."

I half-turned in the chair and looked up at her.

"I know. I'm not worried about anything. I'm just thinking about the old times. Reminiscing mostly—seems like the world is changing so fast. I don't know where I fit in anymore."

"Oh, come on now. You fit in right where you are. Right here with me."

I rubbed her hands. "Your hands are cold, Jesse," I said. "Please don't worry about me—I've just been feeling a little strange lately. That's all. It'll pass."

She rubbed her cheek against mine. "Hey, why don't you make a tee-time with some of your friends," she asked. "You haven't played golf at the club in months. They say the remnants of this hurricane are going to move out tomorrow— it's supposed to be 75 and sunny on Friday. You might as well get some use out of that membership while we're still down here. You know your partners are going to want you back in New York soon."

Oh yeah, I almost forgot about the country club membership that cost me a hundred grand. Did she have to bring that up? Just another one of those things I wish I'd never done. That and this seven-thousand square-foot ocean-front money pit. I've got to give Jesse credit though. She didn't want it. She told me she didn't think we needed a house this big. And she never did like the neighborhood or the country club crowd for that matter. Too uppity she said. I should have listened to her. I'm the one who pushed for it. What was I thinking?

And how the hell did we end up in Miami, of all places? And for seven years! My god! This was supposed to be a two-year gig. Life can sure take you for a wild ride—

especially in my line of work—private equity. Oh yeah, it was a good move. Greg thought it would be a good idea for me to be here. Would give us good proximity to the Latin American telecom market, he said. And he was right.

But now it was payback time for me: lots of stock options, and my turn to get back to the city—I'll do better when I get back up north where I belong.

"Come on in now, will you?" Jessica said, snapping me back from my drifting thoughts. "It's late, and it's windy out here and I'd like to have you next to me as I fall asleep."

Of course it was a reasonable request. So I followed Jessica in and washed up quickly and slipped on some fresh cotton boxers. She was waiting, and I knew from the look on her face we weren't finished with the conversation.

I was right. Jessica said it might be a good idea for the whole family to go back to my hometown to spend the Christmas holidays. By that time, she explained, she hoped her energy level would be back to something close to normal. The doctors had said it would be good for her to get away, if she felt up to it. She thought she would be feeling up to it. And she thought a trip to be with family for Christmas was just what we all needed.

"It will be good for you to be with your family for the holidays," she said, as we lay next to each other. "Besides, it's been a long time since we've been back for Christmas— it's been fifteen years."

I brushed my hair off of my forehead. "No, it hasn't been that long, has it?"

"I'll bet it has. I think the last time we were there for Christmas was the year after Thomas was born. And you know—you haven't even been back there since Albert's..."

"I don't want to talk about that," I snapped.

My response came out stronger than I'd meant it to. Jesse was hurt.

"Alright, Joe," she said. "All I'm saying is that it would do us all good to spend time with family and old friends this Christmas."

I didn't want to talk about Albert. I didn't want to talk about anything. I wanted to let the liquor ease me into a night's oblivion. I took a deep breath and rested my hand in hers. "I'll think about it, Jesse. Anyway, I'll have to check my schedule at work. Let's get some sleep, okay?"

Jessica rolled over and turned away from me. She turned out the bedside light. I lay there in the dark for a few minutes languishing in my remorse. Finally I made a feeble attempt to repair the damage.

"I dreamed of him a while ago," I whispered. "I never told you about it. I dreamt I was pulling him out of some sort of black water. It was really strange Jesse, and so real." I rolled on my side and touched her shoulder. She didn't move.

"Hey, are you asleep?"

~

Frankly, I hoped if I didn't get back to her about the trip she'd just quietly abandon her plans as she had so many times before. I didn't want to go. But Jessica persisted. We argued mildly about it for a few weeks until finally, as usual when she decided to take a firm stand on something, she won.

By the first week of December we had made the arrangements, booked the flights for ourselves and the kids, and contacted the relatives to make sleeping arrangements. They wouldn't hear of us spending the night in a hotel. Jessica and Caryn and I would stay at Paul and Nancy's house. And John and Thomas would stay next door at cousin Jim's. The plans were made. I set my sights on a traditional family Christmas Eve bash.

Appointment confirmed.

THE BLIZZARD

The days of early December flew by, and before long it was time for our trip. Jessica and I and our youngest, Thomas, loaded our bags and drove to the airport. The other two kids, our oldest child Caryn, and middle son John, coordinated their flights from their respective colleges to arrive within a half-hour of us, planning to rendezvous with us at the airport. Our plan was to meet there, rent an SUV, and drive to Paul's house together.

But that was not to be. As fate would have it, weather conditions changed abruptly. Paul called just as we were leaving Miami to tell me the weather report said it was going to be snowing octopus and squid. A storm system moving south from Canada was expected to drop mounds of snow along the southern shores of the Great Lakes and disrupt flight schedules.

Luckily, our flight arrived on time in late afternoon before the storm hit. But John and Caryn weren't so lucky. Their flights were delayed, so they decided they would wait for each other at the airport and drive up together later that day.

We loaded our bags into the rental car and got on the road. I drove as fast as I dared, trying to outrun the storm. But we hit the snow about twenty miles from Paul's house.

As we drove along the shores of the lake, heaps of snowflakes the size of maple leaves dropped from the sky and clung to our windshield before being swatted away by the hypnotic swish of the wipers.

A couple of times, I couldn't see the road for the whiteness of it, and I had to pull over until the deluge slowed down. We passed a few cars that had slid off the road and onto the shoulder. We kept going. There wasn't a lot of choice. It was as bad behind us as it was ahead. But, nerves frazzled, I pulled the car into Paul's driveway around six o'clock. It was already dark. Paul's wife, Nancy, waved us in from just inside the front door.

"Hi you guys! You brought us a white Christmas. First one in four years!" she yelled, as we felt our way up the driveway toward the front porch steps. "You better get in here quick before you get covered in snow."

Nancy held the door open. Like always, her pretty face, milky white skin, and bright blue eyes, brought a lively energy to the room. We walked in, stomping our shoes on the doormat, kicking off slush and snow.

"It's been a long time since I've seen snow like this," I said, giving her a kiss on the cheek and looking around for Paul. "It reminds me of when I was kid."

Thomas and Jessica brushed the snow off their shoulders. Just then Paul sauntered in. He'd come around the corner from the hallway that led to the bedrooms. He tugged at his pants, pulling them up around his waist. He rested one hand on his hips, while the other rested on his round belly.

He looked at us and smiled. "It's about time you got here! Merry Christmas!" he said.

Before I could reply, Nancy stepped behind me and wrapped her arms around Jessica. Jessica melted into her. I looked at Paul and he looked back at me. He knew Jessica's prognosis was dicey.

"I wouldn't have even known you'd been sick, Jesse! You look great!" Nancy said, and she released Jessica from the hug.

Jessica let out a sigh, tightened her lips and looked down at the floor. I knew Nancy meant well. I also knew Jessica wanted to change the subject, to avoid having to talk about her condition. "It's been a long road," is all she said.

Silence hung in the air for a while until Nancy spoke again. "Oh, I'm so glad you're here." She grabbed Jessica's arm and looked over her shoulder at Thomas and me. "Let's get you guys something to drink. Paul, why don't you help the boys to some goodies?"

Thomas and I walked into the dining room with Paul. A platter of cheese and crackers, a bowl of olives, a bottle of wine chilling in a metal bucket, and a bottle of whiskey rested on the white table cloth. A wreath of green cut-pine boughs and glowing ivory-colored candles, made the scene look like a picture in a magazine.

We picked at the food while Nancy motioned for Jessica to follow her through the doorway to the family room.

"We'll let the men talk about football or something," she said. We'll relax and get caught up. We have a lot to talk about." Jesse gave me a glance I couldn't read. Or maybe I could read it pretty clearly. Then she followed Nancy through the door.

"You ladies go right ahead," Paul said.

He stepped toward the table, ignored the bottle of wine in the ice bucket, and opened the bottle of whiskey. He poured three glasses and handed one to me and one to Thomas.

"It's good to see you," he said, as he raised his glass, "Salute!"

Salute. It was old hometown slang. A play on the toast, salud—to your health. It had been awhile since I'd heard that one.

As we talked, I looked around the room. Things had sure changed, I thought. When we were kids, Paul and Albert and I used to play on the floor here with our little, green plastic army men. Then I heard the weather report on TV— more snow was coming. I thought about the kids driving in.

Paul clanged his glass against Thomas's, then mine, tilted his head back, and with one gulp, threw it down. He turned toward the front window just as lights from a car lit up the driveway.

I moved closer to the window. "It's not the kids, is it?" I asked. I knew they couldn't possibly be here already. But I'd been fretting about their making that drive, especially since the storm hadn't let up. I hoped they'd call when they reached the airport, so I could tell them to find a hotel and drive in the next morning. It would be a tough sell—they were eager to get here.

"No," Paul said. "It's Mike. He's come by to pick us up. We're heading down to The Pub. Some of the old gang is in town. They want to see you, Joe—I don't know why." He smiled to let me know he was joking, and slapped me on the back.

Oh great, I thought, the Eagle's Nest Pub, best workingman's bar in town. I hadn't been there in a while. But what the hell, I could use a good stiff drink right about now. Calm the nerves.

Paul turned back toward the table and looked at Thomas. "You coming with us, Tom?"

Thomas swung his long wavy brown hair out of his eyes with a slight swing of his head.

"No thanks, I think I'll stay here and wait for my brother and sister to get in."

"Okay," Paul said. He yelled toward Jesse and Nancy. "Joe and I are headed to The Pub. We'll be back in a little while." He pulled some of his winter gear from the coat closet: a dark blue parka with zip pockets in front, a black knit hat, and black fleece gloves.

"Hey, it's good to have you here for the holidays. It's been a long time since you've been back for Christmas. You know, it hasn't been the same around here at Christmastime since Albert's…"

"Not now, Paul," I said. "I'm not up for that, okay? Let's go have that drink."

Paul got the message. He tossed the parka and hat at me. "Here, you might need these. You're not in the tropics anymore." He raised an eyebrow and smirked. The same way he did when we were kids. Funny how some things never change. "We have snowstorms up here. Did you forget?"

No, I hadn't forgotten. I hadn't forgotten anything that happened here—most of it so far away from everything I had become.

Paul opened the door. A gust of snow blew in.

"Have fun you guys. And be careful!" Nancy yelled. "There's a lot of snow on the roads and lots more coming. Don't stay out too late, okay? We don't want to have to send the dogs out looking look for you."

"Don't worry. We'll be back before midnight," Paul answered.

We ducked our heads against the storm and pushed our way into the cold.

THE PUB

The Eagle's Nest was crowded that night. And although I hadn't been there in over ten years, the pub looked almost exactly like it had the last time—a time warp from the mid-seventies. As soon as I walked in the door, I saw Ben Simpson, an old friend from my Little League days, standing at the bar.

"Oh my god—Joe St. John. I haven't seen you in years," he said. "Get over here and let me buy you a drink." He swung his arm around me and pulled me to the bar. Next thing I knew I was downing a shot of tequila. Not bad, I thought—I hadn't had one of those in a long time.

Ben was almost half a foot taller than me. His thick brown hair and broad shoulders made him look younger than he was. He slapped me on the back a few times and made some small talk and then started yakking about the time our high school baseball team went all the way to the state finals and had the game won until Mark Fedderson let a routine ground ball—which would have been the last "out" of the game—bounce between his legs. Ben shook his head. "All he had to do was catch it, step on third base, and we'd have been state champs!"

Two runs scored and we lost that game in the last inning. We were seventeen years old then, and Ben was still talking about it. I don't think he ever forgave Mark. Funny how some guys never grow up. Ben nodded to Mark who was standing across the bar. I hoped Mark couldn't read Ben's lips. Ben proceeded to tell me about his life—how his daughter had just had a baby girl, and how his two sons were doing well in business.

I don't know if it was the shots of tequila or all the noise in the crowded smoky bar but at some point I tuned Ben out and drifted off, thinking about my kids driving in the snow. Maybe I shouldn't have come here with Paul and Mike. Maybe I should have stayed at the house and waited for them to make it in. I downed another shot of tequila. Oh well, Jessica could handle it.

Ben kept talking and I nodded and pretended I was listening but as I looked at the picture of Danny that had hung above the fireplace mantle for years, I drifted away and thought about him and the old times.

The Eagles Nest Pub got its name from the original owner: Danny "Eagle Eyes" Ferrari. Back in the day we used to just call it "The Pub" and that's what most of the people in town still called it. The old-timers said Danny got the name Eagle Eyes because he had perfect vision. And since he loved to play baseball his perfect vision served him well. He could hit just about anything. He was one hell of a ball player. One hell of a hitter. No matter how hard a pitcher could throw or how much junk a pitcher had, Danny could hit it.

They said he held the all-time, all-state record for least amount of strike-outs in a single season: one. I don't think anybody really checked the record books on that one but the stat sounded good and it added to Danny's reputation.

He could read a license plate a mile away, people said.
Obviously, more home-town lore, but everybody loved
Danny and I guess people just like to believe things that
can't possibly be true because it makes them feel good.

Danny was drafted by the St. Louis Cardinals and
played one year in the majors before he got hurt. When he
opened the bar in the early 50's dock workers and railroaders
hung out in droves. The story goes that one night the wife
of a man who lived next door to the pub called the cops to
complain that a group of men were being noisy and rowdy.
She was probably just tired of her husband coming home
drunk every Friday night. She told the cops there were
"more men hangin' around that place on Friday nights
after work than hornets buzzin' around a hornet's nest."

Word got out about the incident and for a while folks
called the place Danny's Nest. After a while it was known
as Danny Eagle's Nest. Finally it became The Eagle's Nest
Pub, and then, just The Pub. That name stuck. Old Eagle
Eyes put up a lighted outdoor sign with a picture of a great
big soaring blue eagle with huge white eyes that you could
see all the way to the harbor.

When Danny hit eighty-five he got cancer in one eye
and had to have it removed. Soon after that he lost his
vision in the other eye. Go figure. Eagle Eyes can't see
anymore. The locals said he got the cancer from all the
second-hand smoke in the bar. Danny deserved a better
fate. He sold the pub two years ago just before he died, to
my old buddy Fred, a retired fireman looking for a way to
make a few extra bucks. Fred got a gold mine. He made a
pretty good living off it for a guy who never went to college.
He hung a picture of Old Eagle Eyes above the fireplace,

right between Danny's two favorite entertainers: Frank
Sinatra and Dean Martin.

When we were in high school, before we were old
enough to drink, we'd sneak into the pub and Danny
poured us shots of whisky and served us up some cold
beers. That was back in the day when you could do that
sort of thing without somebody blowing the whistle.

The Eagle's Nest had the look and feel of an English
pub. Dark wooden paneled walls and dim lights and a big
fireplace. A big horseshoe-shaped bar of polished mahogany
filled almost the entire bar area. On one side of the fireplace
was a small room with a pool table. Sometimes the pool
table was used for crap games. Danny's office was behind
the pool room.

The pub was packed that night with the old hometown
gang and high school friends and even some guys from
grammar school. I probably knew more than eighty percent
of the people in the bar by name. A few were throwing
darts in the corner and others were singing Christmas
carols. A few were walking around slapping each other on
the back; laughing and carrying on: smoking cigarettes,
chomping cigars, going outside to get high.

Mark Fedderson staggered over to Ben and me. He
ordered three more shots of tequila. Mark had married my
childhood sweetheart Maria—who was more like a sister
than a girlfriend, really—shortly after high school. Mark
had a string of bad luck that started about five years earlier
when he lost his only child—a daughter—to leukemia. And
then he lost Maria three years after their little girl's death,
she died in her sleep. An aneurism, the doctors said.

After Maria's death, Mark went through a rough patch. Just this past summer though, he remarried. I thought about Maria briefly and that strange dream I had about her just before she died. I hadn't thought about that in a while—must have been the tequila. We toasted Mark's recent marriage.

I snapped back from my thoughts just long enough to throw back the shot, and then began to worry about the kids again. Maybe I should call Jesse and see if they made it in, I thought.

But I didn't.

The Voice

I drank way too much that night. No doubt about it —
too many shots of tequila. Not my usual spirit, but it seemed
to be the thing the guys were into drinking those days. It
was late, or early, depending on your point of view. At a
certain point I realized that most everyone was gone. Just
a few stragglers still sitting at the bar. It was time for me to
get back to the house. Jessica probably wondered what
had happened to me. Paul left hours ago.

I was surprised Jessica or Nancy or one of the kids
hadn't called. Or maybe they did. Oh damn, I'd left my cell
phone in the car. Maybe they tried the bar phone.
Bartenders in this hard-drinking part of the country are
trained to be discrete about who's there and who's not,
especially when it comes to the wives. I wasn't really sure
how I got to be one of the last in the bar, or why Paul left
without me. Then I remembered: Paul tried to get me to
come with him. Tried to get me to stop drinking, for that
matter. He must have just given up, and gone home,
thinking I would call for a ride if I needed to.

The fire was still burning. Bruce Springsteen's "Thunder
Road" was on the jukebox. I looked at my watch, but I
couldn't quite see the hands on that expensive piece of
silver and gold machinery. "Hey…" Oh god, I forgot the
bartender's name. And he owned the joint. He was a guy I

went to high school with, for Christ's sake. "Uh…hey, got the time?"

"It's almost three," he said. "I'll be closing up soon. Hey Joe, don't you have some family to go home to tonight?"

I ignored the comment as being impertinent. What the hell is a high school graduate bartender doing saying something like that to me? I fished a fifty from my pocket. "This do it?" The barkeep, whatever the hell his name was, just nodded.

I walked toward the door. Fred, oh yeah, his name was Fred, barked out something that sounded like "Merry Christmas."

I glanced at Fred, then saw the clock next to the Budweiser sign. Sure enough—almost three. How'd that happen? I turned away and pushed on the old wooden door. The wind and snow pushed back harder, and the door crashed inward. Whoa! It was windy. I jumped back just in time to avoid a bloody nose, but I took a knock on the side of my head instead of being hit straight on. I pushed again, putting my shoulders into it. The door swung open, and I staggered out into the parking lot. Two cars still there were covered in snow. They looked like slightly melted, giant blocks of vanilla ice-cream: the kind that comes in a box.

The temperature had dropped even more. The snow was crackly and crunchy. Did Paul leave me the keys for one of these cars? Is that how I was supposed to get home? I felt around in one of my coat pockets for keys.

Snow swirled around the hazy yellow glow of streetlights. Streetlights dangled from slanted wooden poles and swayed back and forth in the wind. No sign of life anywhere: just me, the snow, and the lights.

It was a good thing I knew this part of town. I could vaguely make out the sidewalk by the line of dark trees and the Christmas lights on the shrubs outside some of the houses nearby. As I turned in the direction of one of the cars, I heard something. A quiet little voice. It sounded like it said, *"Walk."*

What? I turned around, but no one was there. Did Fred yell something from the door of the pub? I squinted through the snow. The heavy, dark door was still closed, and I saw a flicker of light from the fire through the frosted windows. Who said that? Ah hell, it's probably just the wind. But then I heard it again.

"Walk back to the house. It's not that far."

Again I turned around. Nothing. Nothing at all. The streetlights barely made an impression against the dark. But wait—was there something moving up ahead, or was it just a bush, tossed into human shape by the wind?

"Walk. Come on now. Walk."

There's that voice again. Am I having DT's? No, it's real this time. "Who the hell are you?" I yelled.

I followed the voice. And I walked. I walked along a sidewalk that appeared recently shoveled. When the sidewalk ended, I switched to the part of the road that looked like it was plowed a while ago. I walked, invigorated by the snow and cold. Then something caught my eye again. What was that? A bush isn't going to be moving ahead of me at a steady pace. Was it a person?

Instead of heading for Paul's house, I followed the barely perceptible figure down a path between two buildings. I walked into an open field near an abandoned railroad yard. What am I doing, I thought. I've got to get back to the house. It's late. I was about to turn back when I saw it again. Something moving about fifty yards ahead of me: this time there were two figures running in the snow.

Were they playing a game? I couldn't see anything through the snow. And the images seemed to get closer, then fade away. But then I saw that they were two little boys, running and hopping around.

What the hell! What are two little boys doing outside in this weather, at this hour? Good Lord, who are their parents? Inebriated as I was, I realized someone had to do something. I tried to move closer, each foot now feeling like a cinder block as I pulled it through the deep and icy-crusted, heavy snow. With each step, my feet sank further.

The wind blew snow globs against my cheeks, and into my eyes. Just barely, I saw one of the boys holding something. A branch? No, wait! I thought. It looked like a rifle. A toy? A carved wooden rifle? Who had those anymore? I hadn't seen one of those since Albert and Paul and I used to play "Cowboys and Indians" when we were little, then, later, after the World War II movies came out, "army"—good guys against the bad guys—my oldest brother Jake taught me that. I always wanted to be one of the good guys.

Just like the three of us used to do, one of the boys pretended to shoot the other, who spun around, and fell down dramatically. He lay in the snow and laughed. Then he flapped his hands and feet to make a snow angel. But that was just how Albert used to...

Hey wait a minute. The boy stood and turned toward me. He motioned for me to come closer. I took a step. He laughed. Did he just call out my name?

"Albert is that you?" I yelled. The boys laughed, then turned away and ran. I hesitated for a moment, unsure of what I was seeing, unsure of what I was feeling. Then I tried to run after them. My legs dragged through the snow. The wind blew. The images faded in and out. I was disoriented: tequila running around inside my brain.

"Hey wait," I yelled. "Who are you? Come back! Where do you live? Come back — you shouldn't be out here alone!" No matter what, I was still a father. I spent the earlier part of the evening, before I got too numb to think about anything, worrying about my own kids driving through this storm. But these kids...something old stirred in me. Something from the time I was a teenager and I always, always, worried about Albert.

I stumbled and my hat fell off. I tried to pick it up, but my gloves were stiff and nearly frozen. "Goddamnit," I yelled. I pulled them off and threw them into the snow. But my hands were too cold to grasp anything, and the clothing had frozen to the surface almost instantly. I couldn't pick up anything.

The two boys ran and laughed and called out to me to come and play with them. But no matter how hard I tried, I couldn't get close. I was confused and exhausted and tired, and I wanted to go home and sleep. But I couldn't leave them out there. I yelled out again, "Wait! Where are you going? Slow down. Let me catch up!"

I tried to quicken my pace but my legs wouldn't move any faster. The boys appeared and faded, appeared again and disappeared. What the hell am I doing out here? I'm drunk, it's three in the morning and I'm out in the middle of a field. Maybe the whole thing is just some weird tequila-induced hallucination.

Then something cracked. I looked down.

It was the sound of cracking ice and — maybe — wood? And then the ground gave way. I fell through a sheet of ice and hardened snow. I rolled through cold black nothingness. I tried to grab something, anything. I tumbled. I slid. I rolled and cracked one leg, and then the other on something solid. I hit my head on cold, hard ice.

I gasped for air. Then slowly my awareness faded.

I was out of it for a few minutes. Or had it been hours? I didn't know. When I came to, it was dark. Black. I was sober and cold and wet. Holy shit! What just happened? I must have fallen through the ice into a cave, or some sort of recess in the ground. Burning and stinging pain coursed through my legs. They're broken, I told myself.

"Anybody out there?" I yelled.

Of course there was no one out there. I was a drunken idiot chasing ghosts from the past. I was buried in the snow. I struggled to pull myself out, tried to dig my way upward with my hands. But there was no leverage. Nothing really to hold onto. Slowly I understood: I was trapped. I was in the middle of a field, in some sort of a hole, and no one knew where I was. My thoughts bounced against each other in panic: What am I going to do? How am I going to get out of here? Oh my god, am I'm going to die? My cell phone? Was it in my pocket? Ah shit, I left the thing in the goddamn car.

But the panic began to seep away. A slow, lazy drowsiness flowed over me. This is what happens when you freeze to death, I thought. You just fall asleep and never wake up. But I wasn't ready to sleep. I wasn't ready to let go. Not yet.

I forced myself to stay awake. What was it I used to do when I was driving late at night, and wanted to keep going despite the incipient sleepiness? I'd find an "oldies" radio station. Turn the music up full-blast, and sing along — yelling out those words.

I slapped myself on the cheeks. No music here though, tough luck, but I hit myself with hard, stinging slaps that brought the blood back to both my face and hands. I took a deep breath. Some songs — could I keep myself awake by singing? Oh shit. Don't sing. Pray. Sing out that prayer: *Hail Mary full of grace the Lord is with thee, blessed art thou…*

Come on now. Stay awake. You can do it. Don't fall asleep. It's going to be okay. Someone will find you.

…amongst woman and blessed is the fruit of…

Okay, that's good. Stay with it. Yell it out. Scream it out. Stay awake.

No. Don't fall asleep. Fight it. Fight it. But it's so damn cold.

Blessed is the fruit of thy womb, Jesus. Holy Mary…

Oh Jesus, help me.

~

What happened? How long have I been in here? I can't see, it's so dark. And what about the kids? Did they make it in? What time is it? It's gotta be after three. Wait, it's getting warm. Oh yeah, there's a light up ahead. Gotta get to it. Is that a tunnel? Oh yeah, a tunnel and a light. Gotta get closer to the light. Is that a fire? Yes, yes, it's a fire! Warm and bright. No, don't go there. Stay awake. Stay in the dark. Don't go to the light. Stay in the dark. Stay awake. But it's so damn cold. What's that sound?

THE LIGHT PLACE

Soft, soft, music. I hear the most wonderful music ever. The voice of an angel. If angels really do exist. Slowly the cave fills with a soft glow, like the morning of a new day. This has to be a dream, I think. I close my eyes. Open them. Blink a few times and there he is: a little boy sitting against the cave's wall.

How did he get in here?

He hugs his knees against his chest. A mop of wavy golden hair falls to just below his eyebrows. Bright, emerald green eyes shine from underneath layers of hair. An orange scarf draped around his neck covers his chest, and pools in soft folds at his feet. His small mouth shapes the sounds and notes of music.

"Who are you?" I ask.

The boy stops singing.

"It's my turn to hide now," he says, in a voice so pure and soft I'm not entirely sure he has actually spoken.

"What did you say?"

Is this the child I was following, I wonder? He's about the same size, and he looks close to the same age. Six, maybe seven?

I look at the smooth and silky walls glistening in the light.

"What did you say to me?" I ask again.

He doesn't respond. He rubs the back of his head, and stares at me. "It's my turn to hide," he says. He glances toward an opening in the cave that I hadn't noticed before, a small opening on the side where the light comes in.

"Is that how you got in here?" I ask.

He doesn't respond. He doesn't look at me. It's as if we're having separate conversations. "Start counting!" he says.

This kid's beginning to irritate me. He's beginning to irritate me a lot. I don't have time for this. "I'm not playing a game," I bark. "I've broken both my legs. I need help. I need to get out of here before I freeze to death."

"Why don't you just get up and walk out?" he asks.

This kid is no help, I think. With the backs of my arms and my hips, I push against the ice around me, and manage to leverage myself against the side of the cave.

"Look, kid. You've got to pay attention to what I'm saying to you. Listen to me, and stop messing around with the back of your head," I tell him.

And with that, he stops. He reaches into the snow and shapes a handful of snow into a geometric design with lacy spires and extensions, glittery like a Christmas ornament snowflake. He tosses it gently back and forth between his two small hands.

"What are you doing?" I ask.

He shoves the molded snow into the chest pocket of his jacket and looks at me.

I try again. "Apparently you don't understand what's happened," I say. "I'm trapped here. I can't move my legs. No one can hear me. No one will be able to find me."

"That's silly, I found you," he says. "You weren't that hard to find. You have to be better at hiding if you want to win this game. Do you want to play or not?"

I whip my head back and forth to wake myself up. I can't believe I'm having a conversation with a child in the light of day, when just a few moments ago it was dark and I was freezing and in pain.

"It's my turn to hide now. Start counting," he says. "And when you get to ten, you try to find me. If you find me, you'll get something really good." The little boy taps the pocket where he put the snowflake. "That's how we play the game."

This damn kid thinks we're playing hide and seek, I realize. Did he fall into the cave with me and suffer a concussion?

"Your leg is okay," the boy says. "Just try it. You'll see."

I touch my leg, gently, gently. Then I bend it slightly. It doesn't hurt anymore.

He smiles. Then he crawls out through the opening.

"Start counting," he says.

ALBERT

Albert sat alone and watched a bird land on the railing of the front porch. Albert didn't move. He just watched. Then he lifted his arm, up toward the bird. The bird twitched, moved its head, side to side. Albert held his arm steady and closed his eyes. Albert was eleven. I was eight.

I wondered what he was thinking. Did he know I was watching from inside the house? Maybe he sensed me there. He told me he could do that sometimes. Maybe he sensed me the way he sensed some people's thoughts. He said sometimes he knew what people were going to say before they said it. I told him I thought he was lucky. I told him I thought he could do a lot of stuff with that. I told him I thought he could use that ability to his advantage. Mom said I was always looking for the advantage. She said Albert doesn't understand what it means to have an advantage.

He wasn't like me. I found that out for sure that day his mother brought him over to our house. Albert stayed outside and sat on the porch. He was waiting for me to come out and play. His mother sat with my mother and cried. She told my mother all about Albert's problem. I listened for a while.

Afterwards, they told me they were counting on me to look out for him. They said he had some kind of condition. I knew something was wrong because he had been twitching and moving his arms and hands around in a weird way more than usual lately. He twitched just like the head of that bird I was watching on the porch railing. He'd done it as long as I could remember. But it seemed to be worse lately, and Albert's mom said it probably wasn't going to get better.

Albert doesn't learn the way most kids learn, his mother said. He's a little slow. I knew he was smart though, just not in the usual way. He was going to start going to a new school for special kids in a few weeks. Some kind of happy school. Now they know he's never going to be a regular grown up. I wondered what they meant by that. His mother had a funny name for his condition that I can't remember. It didn't matter. Albert was my cousin and he was one of my best friends. And that wasn't going to change because of some condition.

Albert looked like a normal kid. His face was round and happy. He smiled a lot. He was bigger than me and Paul. Mom said he was husky. He was the oldest of the three of us: two years older than Paul, three years older than me. Albert was strong. He had big strong muscles on his arms and legs, and a big barrel chest. He was clumsy and awkward though. Sometimes he had a hard time defending himself. Sometimes the neighborhood kids picked on him. But Paul and I were usually there to stick up for him.

Albert liked to play baseball. He couldn't catch like Paul and me. But he could hit the ball a mile. So we usually let him hit clean-up when we played ball in the field down the street.

The bird fluttered its wings and flew up, off the railing. Then, wow! — it landed right on Albert's arm. Albert held still. He whispered something to the bird. Were they talking to each other? I wondered. Albert jerked his arm ever so slightly. The bird jumped off. Albert watched the bird fly away.

THE LIGHT PLACE

Start counting? Did the little boy hear anything I said? I'm hurt and I have to get out of here. I weigh the mounting odds against me and decide I have to do something. So in spite of the absurdity of my situation, I follow the little boy's instructions and begin counting.

One…Two…Three…By the time I reach ten I'm able to move both my legs without any pain. I roll over onto my hands and knees and crawl out through the opening which, strangely enough, is now large enough for me.

And then I'm warm. I stand and look for the little boy. No sign of him anywhere. Mountains and valleys stretch into the distance forever. The mountains are covered in white. It's snowing, but the snow is neither cold nor wet. I try to catch the snowflakes. Dozens land on my hand. They don't melt. They disappear.

To my side, a sun sinks below the horizon, sending streams of orange and lavender across the sky. On the other side, a disc rises in a shimmer of spreading yellow that overlaps in layers across the lavender glow.

Almost without thinking, I take a step forward, on legs I thought were broken. Not far from where I'm standing, a cottage of field stone in shades of brown nestles in the snow, surrounded by pines and willows, their snow-laden branches drooping like thick strands of white, coarse hair.

The cottage has two chimneys. Pale smoke wafts into the orange and lavender sky. Past the front door, a shallow stream flows over rounded pebbles and rocks.

I stuff my hands into the pockets of my parka even though they aren't really cold.

Yellow light pours from small windows. A wreath made of something like the dark green leaves of magnolia hangs on a lamppost on the other side of the brook, and another just like it is mounted on the cottage door, encircling a brass door knocker. The door is shaded by an awning.

This isn't my hometown. This isn't any place I've ever seen.

I cross the stream on a stone bridge. At the cottage, I step onto the door stoop, but before I can knock, the door opens. A woman stands in the doorway.

She's wearing a rose-colored dress, a beige linen apron, and a robin's-egg blue scarf draped around her shoulders. Her auburn hair falls to just above her shoulders and she stands straight and erect. She has a white powdery substance on one cheek. Her eyes are green. When she smiles her red lips part in what seems to be an expression of joy.

"Finally!" she says. "I thought you'd never get here!" She wipes her hands on the apron.

"Do I know you?" I ask. I shift my weight and move my legs back and forth. Just to feel them. To make sure they don't hurt. To make sure they aren't broken.

"I don't know. Do you?" She tilts her head, coquettishly.

"I'm sure I remember you from when I was a boy, or from somewhere else. You look familiar, younger maybe and...please, who are you?

"Ah." She interrupts. "Be patient."

I look into the cottage, and try to calm myself.

Whoever this woman is seems to be lurking just at the edge of my consciousness. But just like that damn kid, the little boy in the cave, I can tell she isn't going to make it easy for me. Okay, I've had it with these people and their games and coyness.

I clench my fists and stand straight and look into her eyes real hard. "Where am I?" I demand.

Her smile grows broader. Teasing, not mocking.

Why is this woman playing a game with me? Does she think this is fun? This is serious. I don't know where the hell I am or how I got here. I want to know what's going on. I'm pissed off.

I take a deep breath and let it out slowly.

"You don't know?" The woman smiles.

"Oh come on now—no, I don't know. I walked in a snowstorm in a field. I saw two boys playing. I chased after them. I fell through the snow. I was trapped in some kind of crevice or snow cave. It was dark and cold and I thought I was going to die. Then I heard a little boy singing. He told me he was playing a game. Right now I just want to get out of here. My family is waiting for me at Paul's house. Look, could you just help me out here?"

Surely I must be dreaming. I tap my fist on the brown stones a few times. Solid.

"He has something for you."

I roll my eyes and sigh. "So is this some kind of game?" I hear a sound and turn toward it. I could swear I saw that little boy run by. I look back at the sky and the shimmering colors and the landscape and it's all so beautiful and peaceful, and my irritation drains from me because I simply can't hold it with all this beauty around me. Okay, I think, I know it's a cliché, but have I died and gone to heaven?

Did I just hear someone say something? I turn back to the woman.

"It's so beautiful," I whisper. "The light here is…"

"Yes. The light is." she says.

She steps outside to stand on the stoop next to me. She wraps the scarf gently around her neck.

"I must be dreaming. But if this is a dream, you sure seem real." I whisper.

The woman looks at me and I could swear she says something but her mouth doesn't move. Did she actually say the words—"the light place?"—or did I imagine it? Or was it me who came up with those words later? Nothing makes sense. But standing here on the doorstep with this woman I almost remember, it's as if certain things enter my mind on their own—spoken or unspoken—and somehow I'm being told that I'm returning to a place I once inhabited a long time ago.

I look beyond the woman, into the room, and see a stone fireplace that crackles and flares; red and orange flames make shadows on the walls. And I smell the most wonderful aroma.

"I know that smell. That's…"

Her eyes open wide. "Remember now?"

And then memories come rushing in and I realize I've been holding my breath.

She smiles. "I told you I would see you again."

1954

I think the fire dreams started when I was five. I didn't remember them at first. I just woke up crying. They happened only occasionally in the beginning, every couple of months. But by the time I was six, I was having them once a month or more, and remembering them all. It was almost always the same, something like this:

> *I'm standing in the basement of my house.*
>
> *I'm small, smaller than the furniture in the room. There's a brown box on the floor by a table. A lady with long black hair and a black dress lights the lantern on the table. She looks like an angel but she's scary. She opens the box and pulls out a package.*
>
> *I ask her, what is it? It's a secret, she says, don't tell anyone. She tries to give me the package. I don't want it. I run away. I run up the stairs and through a room I've never seen before. I run out the front door. I think I'm safe but she follows me down the steps to the lawn and stands next to me. She has a sad look on her face. She holds my hand. I can see inside the house even though the door is closed. Then I see the lantern explode and the house catches fire. I see smoke and flames.*

And then I wake up crying and screaming.

The episodes became progressively worse until one morning after a particularly troubling night, Mother had enough. She was worried about me and her answer to the worry — to most worries actually — was to go see the priest, in the parish building a few blocks away.

I didn't like the priest at first. I don't know why. He was a nice man. Maybe I didn't like his black clothes and the white collar he wore around his neck. Or maybe it was because he always seemed so serious whenever I saw him in Mass. He was an older man, short and round with a red face and a pink bulb nose. He smelled a little funny, like smoke and the whiskey my father drank, mixed together.

We sat in his office in the building next to the church. The room was small and dark with a big wooden desk. Thick red curtains hung around the windows. The priest asked me to sit down in one of the two high-back chairs in front of his desk. He sat next to me in the other. It was just me and him in the room. He had asked Mother to wait outside.

He asked me about my dreams. I made things up. I didn't want to tell him about the fire dream. I wanted to keep the secret just like the woman in the dream said. I didn't want to tell anyone about the dream. I told him my scary dreams were about a wolf chasing me through the woods. I think he knew I was making up a story. I could tell by the way he looked at me: the way his eyes darted back and forth real fast looking at each one of my eyes separately when I talked to him.

Some people look at me that way when I talk to them and it makes me scared. Some people look right into both my eyes when I talk to them. But it only seems that way. They really look into one eye for a while and then they look in the other — but they do it slowly and it seems like they're looking directly into my eyes. They don't scare me, and I usually tell them the truth. Mother looks at me that way. I always tell her the truth—well, most of the time anyway. But even she doesn't know my secret.

The priest and I talked for maybe a long time. Besides the questions about the dreams, he asked me about school, my friends, and my favorite sports. When we finished talking, the priest stood up. I think he expected me to stand up too, but I waited. This might be my last chance to ask him, I thought, so I just sat there and looked up at him.

"What is it, Joey?" he asked. I stared at the floor.

I didn't know if I should ask him or not. But I had to know. "Are angels real, Father Tom?"

Father Tom furrowed his eyebrows and looked at me real hard. It was the kind of look that said: I wasn't expecting that question. "Oh, yes, of course they're real," he said. "Why do you ask?"

I looked away.

"Joey, did an angel come to you in your dream?"

I didn't know why I asked him. Now I had to tell him the truth. I turned my head away and looked out the window. I was almost crying. I tapped my heel on the ground like I was stomping for a bug. "But she told me not to tell anyone, Father."

Father Tom knelt on one knee in front of my chair and looked into my eyes. "Don't worry Joey. I won't tell anyone," he said as he folded his hands on his knee. "Why don't you tell me about the angel in your dream?"

So I told him. I told him about the woman with the black dress. I told him about how she wanted to give me a package but I wouldn't take it. I told him about some other things, and we talked for a little while, but I didn't tell him about the fire dream.

I cried. "It's okay, it's okay, he said. "Don't be afraid. The angel won't hurt you. I think she wants to help you. If she comes again, maybe you can take the package and see what's inside." Father Tom took a clean, white handkerchief from his pocket and put it in my hand. I wiped my face and eyes. I sat in the chair for a little while and Father Tom squatted beside me. He put his hand on my shoulder. "All right, I think we talked enough today, don't you?" He told me again not to be afraid. He didn't ask me anymore questions. He stood and took my hand and together we walked into the room where Mother sat.

~

"Well Carmela, Joey and I had a nice talk. He's a good boy and he's going to be just fine," Father Tom said. Then he looked at me again. His eyes were red and watery. "We all have scary dreams and they're nothing to be afraid of."

I watched his mouth move, barely hearing his words. My thoughts were on the sunshine and the leaves of the trees bouncing in the cool spring breeze. In this room, the drapes were pulled back all the way and the window was opened a little. The sun streamed through the window and I saw tiny specks of dust floating in the sunbeams.

I was thinking about playing with Paul and Albert. I was thinking about the other day when my friend Maria kissed me and said she wanted to be my girlfriend. I wondered what Paul and Albert were doing. Had they started building the fort yet? I told them I would be there to help them. How much longer did we have to stay here?

"Joey, listen! Father is talking." Mother said.

Her voice startled me and snapped me back into the room. "Okay!"

Father Tom looked at my mother as he ushered me over to where she was sitting. My mother pressed him. "But it's been going on for a long time, Father. He wakes up terrified!"

Mother glanced at me. She looked at my hands fiddling around in my pockets. I wondered if she knew I had the pocket knife she told me not to bring.

Father Tom rubbed his hand over his head and looked out the window. Then he glanced at Mother. "He's going to be okay. Children go through phases as they grow. And when worries and concerns come along we must give them to the Lord. Can he recite the 'Guardian Angel Prayer' yet?"

Mother bit her lip. Sometimes she did this when she thought really hard about something. It looked like she was thinking real hard and I expected her to ask the priest another question, but instead she nodded and looked at me. "We say it together sometimes in the morning, don't we Joey? Can you say it for Father Tom?"

Mother smiled. Then she began, "Angel of God my guardian dear…"

I joined in, "To whom God's love commits thee here…"

Father Tom leaned against a bookcase that took up one wall of the room. He closed his eyes and listened as we continued slowly.

"Ever this day, be at my side. To light. To guard. To rule. To guide."

Father Tom joined Mother and me as we said, "Amen." Then he opened his eyes and looked at me. "Ah, that's always been one of my favorite prayers," he said. "Joey, do you ever pray on your own?"

I was tired of being in this room and I wanted to leave. "Yes Father." I answered.

I squeezed the knife in my pocket so hard it hurt my hand.

"Who do you pray to?" He asked.

I was getting mad. "I don't know."

Mother glared at me. She made her neck tight, and opened her eyes real wide like she wanted to give me a thump.

"Jesus." I said. I said that because I knew that's what she wanted me to say.

Father Tom winked at me.

"Oh, that's a good boy. Then ask Jesus to help you have good dreams and say the 'Hail Mary' with your mother before you go to sleep at night." He looked at my mother again. "Why don't you try this and let me know how things go, okay?" He stepped toward the door. "Oh, and say hello to Jack for me, Carmela. Tell him I really appreciate his help with the new building."

Mother nodded and smiled. "Oh sure, he's usually so busy seeing patients, but he loves a chance to pull out his tool-kit when he has the time." she said.

Father Tom looked at me sideways and gave me another wink. Mother and I walked toward the door. She reached for the handle but then took some steps back toward the priest. Father Tom mumbled something to her that I didn't understand. Mother looked at me like she felt sorry for me. We walked out together holding hands.

~

Not long after our meeting with the priest I had a dream about a little girl and a pot of boiling water. The little girl pulled the pot off the stove and the water spilled all over her and she melted. After I had that dream, the fire dreams stopped for a while. But soon I was having them again.

One night, after another fire dream, I woke up crying but I didn't scream. My pillow was wet. Mother didn't hear me that night. She didn't come to my room. So I crept across the hallway to where my mother and father were asleep.

The hallway was dark but there was enough light for me to feel my way along. My brothers were asleep in their rooms. My oldest brother Jake was in the room next to mine, and my other two older brothers, James and Michael shared a room further down the hall.

I knocked on the door. I heard my father's voice. It was muffled-sounding, and tired, but he told me to come in. Mother was still sleeping. I could see the moon through the window by their bed. I walked past the dresser and the chair where my daddy had draped his pants. When I got to the bed my mother woke up.

"What's wrong, Joey? Another bad dream?" she asked, as she sat up and looked at me.

My nose was running and I wiped it on my pajama sleeve.

"Want to get in here with us for a while?" she asked. "Crawl up over me." She pulled the bedspread aside, and reached toward me.

Mother did the same thing she did after my other bad dreams. She hugged me and pulled me close to her and wiped my tears with her nightgown. But that night she didn't ask me about the dream and I didn't tell her anything. I just lay there between her and my father and thought about the angel prayer.

My father rolled over, and patted my arm. "It's okay," he whispered, "Remember, we're going to go out and find that little bunny tomorrow." He put his arms around me and I snuggled next to him. He kissed my head and my whole body warmed. I was safe again.

I fell asleep and the lady I used to call the angel came to me. She raised her finger to her lips.

～

"Shh…whisper," she says. "We don't want to wake them."

She looks like the lady in the fire dream but she's younger and friendlier. She smiles a lot. I lie still and look up at her.

"Watch this," she says.

She shows me a little box.

"What is it?" I ask.

"A surprise!"

She floats above the bed. Then she peeks at my mother and father to make sure they're sleeping.

"A surprise?"

"Yes. Watch. But remember, this is our secret," she whispers. She puts her finger up to her lips. Shh…

I nod my head. "I won't tell."

She floats right in front of me and her dress tickles my nose. She opens the box and throws something high into the air. But it doesn't fall down. It floats. It's a big fluffy ring of smoke like the kind Uncle Lou blows from his cigar when he tries to be funny, and there's something like a "steely" marble in the middle of it.

I giggle. It's silly.

Shh…don't wake up mommy and daddy.

The smoke ring floats to the ceiling and disappears.

The lady waves good-bye and I wake up.

I like this dream better than the other one.

As I fell asleep again, I watched the Christmas lights outside the window. Green and red and yellow bulbs shining dim through the curtains. They clattered against the window when the wind blew. I smelled the smell of fresh cut pine from the Christmas tree down the hall.

THE LIGHT PLACE

The woman in the rose dress holds the cottage door open and guides me into the dim room. A picture of a striped cat curled on a couch hangs above the fireplace. A black-iron gate opens to an outdoor patio with a flower garden, a water fountain, and lush green plants.

How can it be springtime out there? It was snowing before I came in.

She asks me to sit in a leather chair with a green paisley seat cushion. Four chairs surround an oval dining table made of dark, shiny wood. On the table rests a white pot with a curved spout and two white cups. She sits next to me at the table, picks up the pot, and pours something into one of the cups. Steam rises from the cup and spout.

"Be careful, it's hot." She says.

"What is it?" I ask.

"A special brew to help you sleep," she says. She smiles. "Try it."

I know this woman, damn it. I just can't quite figure out who she is. I think I know what's going on here. Maybe. But I'm not dead—yet. Am I? Maybe I'm just visiting.

Just at the edge of my vision I see three candles sitting atop a buffet of cherry-brown wood, a few feet away from a green and red striped sofa.

If I'm visiting maybe I can excuse myself after I drink this "special brew" and get back to Paul's house. I wonder if the kids made it in. Did she say sleep? Oh no, I don't want to do that.

"But I'm not tired." I say.

She smiles at me, oh so slightly, and her lips part, exposing the white tips of her upper teeth. "Of course you are. You've traveled a long way my dear. Take a sip."

A long way? What does she mean by that? No, I really don't want to drink this, especially if it puts me to sleep. But…what? No, she didn't say anything more, did she? I really don't want to drink it. I want to go…but…it smells so good. I really have to…I'm sorry, I can't…

But something compels me to drink. I try to stay in control, but I can't. Okay, I rationalize, just a sip. I don't want to be rude. This woman's obviously gone through some trouble—making me a warm drink and welcoming me into her home. How big is this place anyway? Sure is deceiving. I'll bet it has more square feet than my house. Wouldn't know it from the outside.

I lift the steaming cup to my lips. The warm liquid flows over my tongue. Oddly, a stream of something cool flows down my throat and into the middle of me: a spectrum of colors; liquid starlight. Oh, but that is so good.

She stands and reaches for my hand. "Come with me."

I stand, and nearly stumble. I am so dizzy. "What just happened?" I ask her. "I feel strange. I think I'm going to be sick."

"You're okay, just breathe and walk. Slowly."

She holds my hand, and leads me through a doorway

into a room that I'm sure wasn't there before. Inside the room is an iron-framed canopy bed with primrose–colored covers and white lace pillows. I sit down, but I can't stay upright. I sink into the bed's softness. So sleepy. So sleepy. The pillow is as soft as a dream of meadows. I hear the brook drifting by outside. I feel the weight of a blanket dropped over me. The whisper of a voice. "Sleep."

Lips graze my forehead.

I don't want to sleep. I remember trying to stay awake in the cave, slapping my cheeks, but now the attempt at movement feels like slow motion. I can't help myself. I close my eyes. I begin to dream. But is it a dream? I'm not sure. And what happened to the snow, the ice, the darkness?

∼

First I hear static, like the sound of someone trying to tune in a radio station. Then I hear a voice.

"We'll be back before midnight."

That's Paul's voice!

Then a deeper, more melodious voice. "It's going to be a dandy folks, an Alberta Clipper bringing frigid temperatures from the north down over the warmer waters of the southern Great Lakes. We could see impressive snowfalls. Expect two to three feet of fresh…"

Was that the radio broadcast we heard before we got out of the car at the pub?

"Don't stay out too late…"

Hey! That's Nancy's voice!

"A winter storm warning is in effect for the next forty-eight hours. Don't drive if you don't have to. It's a good night to curl up by the fire or maybe wrap some of those last minute gifts. It looks like we're going to have a white…"

That's the announcer from the television station!

I drift through soothing bands of colors: purple and green and blue, then into a gray darkness. The darkness turns to white and I'm floating like a flake of snow above the pub: slowly, effortlessly, down and down.

Below, barely visible through the storm, three men scramble across the pub's slick parking lot, and bolt for the lighted tavern entrance. It looks like…Paul? And is that our cousin Mike with him, just like last night? And? Who's that other guy? He's wearing a parka and…is the third man me?

I look around the bar, and I see myself again.

I'm leaving the pub and waving good-bye to Fred. The door hits me on my head. I see myself walk down the street into the field next to the old railroad yard. I throw my gloves to the snowy ground. I watch myself fall through the ice and snow.

I float over treetops and snow covered roofs: over the baseball field where I played as a boy, over the cemetery where my family and my friends are buried, over the river where I used to play sometimes without my parents knowing. I float to Paul's house over the trees. Snow drops from the sky and piles on the rooftops, trees, and the ground below.

I float into the kitchen of Paul's house and hover close to the ceiling. Can anyone see me? I don't know. The oak cabinets and the cream colored walls are brighter and more defined than I had ever seen them.

And what's this? Jessica's sitting at the old kitchen table in the middle of the room that I remember so well. Paul and Nancy are there, too. With one finger, Nancy is tracing the squares of the red and white check tablecloth that I know Paul's mother gave her. Jessica is tense and folded into herself, in her white bathrobe and pink nightgown. That's the nightgown I bought for her when she was so depressed and down about the cancer. Silky and form-fitting, feminine but not provocative, it was the right thing at the right moment. She's not wearing her wig, of course. Her close-cropped, light brown hair covers the top of her head. The absence of make-up and the lingering effects of the chemotherapy reveal purple discoloring beneath her eyes.

Coffee cups are strewn across the table, but only Paul has a filled cup. A drip coffeemaker sits half-full on the cream-tiled kitchen counter just behind him.

"Don't worry Jesse," Nancy says. "I'm sure he's fine." She turns to her husband. "Paul, why don't you call Fred and see if he knows where Joe is?"

"I'll bet he slept at the pub last night," she says. She watches Jessica.

"Why would he do that?" Jessica asks, as she turns toward Paul. "I tried his cell phone. But I keep getting his voice mail."

Nancy's hair is pulled into a ponytail. She watches Jessica and waits for Paul to respond. Paul puts his coffee cup down and pushes his chair from the table.

Paul ignores Jessica's comment. "That's a good idea. I'll call Fred." He says.

Nancy watches Jessica and pours coffee into a green mug on the kitchen table. "Fred has an office at the pub with a bed and a shower and a sleeper sofa in it. Sometimes guys crash there if they drink too much. Right, Paul?"

Paul nods.

"He practically lives there," Nancy says. "Especially when he's had too much to drink—and that happens a lot these days." Nancy bends to open a lower cabinet door and pulls out a frying pan. "How about some eggs? I think we should eat."

Jessica frowns and looks at them. She cups her hands over her face and lets her fingers slide down her cheeks to just slightly below her eyes. She takes a deep breath through her nose and slowly lets it out through her mouth as she folds her hands to make a table for her chin.

"Where could he be?" Jessica says, as she looks out the window. "Look at that snow. It's really bad out there. He should have left with you Paul."

∼

Something strikes me at this moment. Something in my awareness shifts. I don't know what I am or what I'm doing or where I'm going. If only I could reach out and touch them and let them know I'm here somehow. But I cannot.

Paul looks at the clock above the kitchen window. He tells Jessica and Nancy what happened at the pub. He moves his lips, but I don't hear the words. I don't hear as one hears sounds, but I hear, or should I say, I sense, in a new and different way.

He tells them that he tried to get me to come home with him, but I refused. He hated to say it, he says, but I got pretty belligerent about it. He figured Fred would call him if I needed a ride

Paul picks up the phone and dials. He's talking with Fred. Then I see him end the call and turn toward the two women.

"Fred said Joe left the bar around three. He left by himself. He said Joe was one of the last ones to leave."

Paul looks at Nancy and then at Jessica. He raises his eyebrows.

"Is he sure about that?" Nancy asks.

Paul nods his head, yes, and frowns. "I think so. He said he would check the parking lot to see if there are any cars out there—might give him a clue."

Paul takes another sip from his mug and sets it back down on the table. He seems rooted in place, as if he doesn't want to take the next step. And I know what he's thinking: He doesn't yet want to admit the possibility, growing stronger every moment, that something bad has happened to me. Or that I am safe somewhere, but don't especially want to be found.

"You'd better call the police, Paul," Nancy says.

Jessica sits up straight in her chair. "I agree, it's time," she says.

I see a movement at the door that leads from the dining room, just a bit of color that for a second seems to have no form. But I know who it is even before my daughter,

Caryn,—thank god she made it—walks into the kitchen rubbing her eyes.

"What's going on in here," she asks. "Call the police about what?"

Paul looks down. He stares at the floor as if he's studying a pattern there. Then he looks up, at Caryn.

"It's your dad. He's not back from the pub yet."

My daughter tilts her head to one side and her eyes go blank for a moment, as if she's suddenly miles away. I recognize the puzzled look on her face from when she was a child. But after a moment, she snaps her attention back to Paul.

"Not back from the pub!" she says. "He must have really tied one on."

Jessica makes what I know is an almost involuntary gesture of denial: one quick shake of her lowered head, and a hand partially lifted to push the thought away. I can see the tears forming in her eyes, and so can Caryn. She pulls a chair from the table and sits next to Jesse, reaches out and takes her mother's hand.

"What happened?" she asks. She looks at everyone in the kitchen, searching for the one who has the answer. "Where is he?" She doesn't know that the person with the answer is floating above her, loving her with all his heart.

Paul runs his hand over the remaining grayish brown hair on the front of his head. He tugs at his drooping blue jeans. "We don't know where he is." Paul says. "But I'm sure he's fine. Maybe he went…"

Nancy springs forward like a coiled snake attacking its prey. "Call the police Paul! It's a damn blizzard out there!

Who knows what happened to him? Maybe he's stuck in the snow somewhere!"

Paul doesn't look at her, or anyone else at the table. He addresses his comment to the wall. "Let's wait until we hear back from Fred."

Caryn tugs and strokes the long strands of her straight, light-brown hair—just like her mother does when she's anxious. "If he's stuck in his car, he could be hurt or freezing." she says.

"He doesn't have a car, sweetie." Nancy says, as she looks at Paul.

The phone rings. Paul walks around the kitchen table to answer it. He mumbles a few words, shakes his head a few times, then looks at the women. "Fred said there's only one other car in the lot besides his and he doesn't know who it belongs to, but there's no sign of Joe."

"Paul, why on earth did you…" Nancy begins, but then thinks better of it. "This is crazy! Where could he be?"

Jessica puts her head in her hands. I can see her trembling. Oh, baby, I'll be all right, I want to tell her. I want to float down to Jessica and wrap my arms around her and say, I'm here, right here in the room with you. But I'm not there. I'm floating above them. But that isn't true either. I'm not sure where I am.

No, rather, I'll tell them, I'm buried in the ice and snow in the middle of the old railroad yard. Or no, I'm sleeping on a soft fluffy bed in a strange place that makes no sense to me. I want to tell them what happened, but I can't. Even if I could, what would I say?

Paul tries hard to be calm and reassuring, I can see that. He sits on the edge of a kitchen chair and bounces his leg against the table like an antsy teenager.

"Maybe he tried to walk back here last night. It's not that far." Paul says.

He gets up from the table and walks to the front room — the living room we call it nowadays. He squeezes his bulk around the Christmas tree to look out the bay window there. The sky outside has begun to lighten. Mounds of snow, blown by the wind, have piled up in uneven layers across the lawn and onto the place where the sidewalk used to be.

"Why would he try to walk back here in this blizzard?" Jessica asks. "And if he did, where is he? Passed out in a snow bank?"

Paul turns from the window. He walks back to the kitchen, picks up the coffee pot and pours the remnants of the pot into his cup. He pauses for a moment, raises a finger to his lips, and nods his head.

"I'm going to go look for him," he says. He slams the cup down.

Caryn stands, biting one of her fingernails. "I'm going with you." she says.

Nancy wipes her nose on some torn, crumpled tissues she pulls from the pocket of her robe. She urges Paul and Caryn not to be foolish, not to venture out in the storm. Once again, she tells Paul to call the police.

But Paul doesn't call the police. Instead he says, "Maybe Joe left the bar with someone and he didn't want Fred or anyone else to know about it." He looks straight ahead — doesn't meet Jesse's eyes.

He's going out to look for me on his own, he tells them. "You guys call the police, if you think that's necessary," he says. He goes into the living room, opens the coat closet. He pulls out a heavy gray coat and buttons it up.

"What are you saying Paul?" Jessica fires. She stands up. "What? You think he left with someone? Is that what you're saying?"

She grips the edge of the table for a few seconds. Then she turns and walks out of the room.

"Jesse!" Nancy calls after her. She shoots Paul a look, scowling. "Paul didn't mean that. I'll call the police. Don't do anything foolish, Paul. The weather's getting worse. Just go find him."

Nancy follows Jessica out of the kitchen and down the hallway.

I try to move closer to Jessica but something holds me back. I'm pulled across the kitchen and through the ceiling and above the roof. I drift upward into the white sky, above the house, above the town, above the clouds. I drift upward until I see the first fleck of sunlight basking the horizon with streams of orange and peach.

Then I'm back on the bed. I open my eyes and look up. Blue and white light pours through the windows. The woman in the rose dress stands near the bed and looks at me.

1955

The dreams persisted and became more vivid. And when the things—the premonitions—started happening about a year later, Mother didn't know what to do. She waited until she couldn't take it anymore. That was her way: suffer the pain as long as possible. It was her motto actually, her way of living. Suffering is God's way of making you a better person, she used to say when we were sick or if something didn't turn out quite right: especially if that something affected one of her children.

Mother said it was noble to suffer. It was good for the soul. But I didn't believe it. Why would God want us to suffer? But Mother suffered with me until she reached her limit with my bad dreams and nightmares. Then it was back to the priest.

Mother and I walked to the church again on a gray, autumn day. My dog, Paddy, ran along behind us, though Mother warned me I would have to leave him outside once we got there. Dusky red leaves, interspersed with orange and yellow, drifted from the trees that lined the street, urged from their branches by the cool afternoon breeze. I kicked at the piles of color along the sidewalk, admiring the carpet they formed across the neighborhood lawns. And it took my mind off what was about to happen. Mother seemed a little nervous, too. She'd changed out of one of her plaid zip-up-the-front housedresses that were her at-home attire, into a "Sunday" dress, even though it was the middle of the week.

If I've given the impression that I didn't like the priest, that's not entirely true. I was afraid of him at first. But as time passed, and I began to know him a little better, I started to like him.

Father Tom greeted us that day in his usual attire: black shirt and pants, and the ever-present white collar. A fat, unlit cigar dangled from the corner of his mouth. We sat in the big room outside his office. Mother was teary-eyed by the time we sat down. My last dream had scared her because I thrashed about for almost five minutes before she could wake me.

She placed her black purse on the floor next to her chair. "Father," she said, "We have to do something. I don't know how much more of this I can take. It happens almost once a week now, he wakes his brothers up with his crying, and it's getting worse. He's had two dreams in the past few months that have come true. He dreams about something and a few days later it happens! It's scaring me, Father."

Mother grabbed her purse and pulled a tissue from it and wiped her eyes. "Oh," she sighed, "I don't know why I get so emotional."

The phone rang on the square wooden table next to Father. He looked at Mother. "Excuse me for a moment," he said. Then he leaned across the table, and answered it.

"Yes, this is he," Father said. He shifted the phone to his other ear. "Oh yes, we should respond to them by the end of the week." He looked at me and winked. "Did you take it to the grounds committee? Well, that's fine." He straightened a stack of Catholic Living magazines with his free hand. "We better talk about this later though. I have someone in my office." He looked at his watch. "Okay, thanks for calling."

Father placed the phone back on the receiver and turned toward Mother. He sat back, crossed his legs and chomped on the cigar a few times before he balanced it on the edge of a black plastic ash tray. He tried to comfort her. "Now Carmela, Joey is going to be fine. Nightmares are quite normal at his age."

Father Tom picked up a Bible that sat near him on the table. He opened it and rifled through the pages as if he were looking for a specific passage. "You know, the Lord has answers for everything, Carmela."

Mother clutched her purse tight against her body. "But father, you don't understand. These are more than just nightmares. Things are happening."

"Here, I want to read something to you." Father Tom stopped skimming and moved his finger to a place on a page. He started to read, but then he paused as if he had changed his mind. "Okay, okay, I know…" He rested his chin in his hand and looked at Mother. "I'm not sure there's much more I can do, Carmela. Have you been praying with him before he goes to sleep?"

"Yes, Father, every night. It's not helping." Tears trickled down her cheeks and she wiped them away as fast as they came. "I don't know what's wrong with me. I can't stop crying. I'm sorry, Father." She pushed her hair away from her eyes. It was a nervous habit. She tugged and twisted the ends of a strand, then tried to quiet her hands by clasping them on her lap.

Father Tom looked at Mother for a long time. Outside, the nearly barren branches tapped against the window. The priest closed the Bible and pushed it back to the place on the table where it had been.

Mother began twisting her hair again. I'd seen her do this before. I'd seen her with this nervousness and anxiety. Like when my brother James had his accident, the day he raced his bike on the street with our cousin. Mother had told us, over and over again, never to race in the street. But James didn't listen.

As they raced through the street, a car careened around the corner. My cousin grabbed my brother's handle bars to try to wrench him out of the way. But James lost control. His bike slid underneath the moving car. The driver slammed his brakes, and the squealing sound carried all the way up the street to our house. My brother's head ended up only inches from the car's tire. Just a few inches more and his head would have looked like a watermelon dropped from a ten story building.

As it was, he had nasty cuts and scrapes on his head and shoulders, and a bruised kidney. Mother said it was an angel that intervened, held out her hand she said, and stopped the car from crushing my brother's head. Was it the same angel that I knew, I wondered?

I remembered how Mother tugged at her hair as we sat in the hospital waiting room outside the emergency room while my father attended to James. That's what she did as we waited for the priest to respond.

Father Tom looked out the window and seemed to study the branch still tapping against the glass. He picked up the cigar from the ashtray, put it in his mouth, struck a match and pulled at it to get the ember going. When the smoke was flowing, he lifted his head toward the ceiling and exhaled, slowly, deliberately. He turned toward us.

"Something's not right," Mother said. "It's not just the nightmares anymore. He's having dreams about things before they happen now. I didn't tell you this before, but you remember the accident with the little girl and the pot of boiling water on the stove? He dreamt about it the night before it happened. I'm frightened for him Father. He sees things in his dreams before they happen."

Mother stopped tugging on her hair and looked at me. She patted my hand.

Father Tom picked up the box of matches on his desk and looked at it. He closed his eyes. Took a deep breath. Then he shook his head before he opened his eyes and looked at Mother.

"Okay, I have something I want to tell you," he said. "I've been praying about this since you called last week to schedule the appointment. Now I know — I'm sure the Lord has guided me. There's someone I want you to meet."

Mother slid her hands over her skirt and let them come to rest on her legs. She leaned forward. "Who is it?" Mother asked. She glanced at me to see if I was listening. I pretended to look out the window.

Father Tom leaned back in his chair. "There's a woman I met a while ago. I think she would be a good person for you to know. She's wise and insightful. It might be good for you and Joey to go see her.

"Does she live around here?" Mother asked.

"Yes," Father Tom said.

"Can you tell me more about her?"

"Well, I met her when she first came to this area about three years ago. She stopped by one day to introduce herself to me at the prompting of an old friend, a priest I met in the seminary, who's a pastor now in a parish in New Mexico.

"She used to live near the river. You know that big white house with the black shutters on River Birch Road?"

"Yes, I know that house," Mother said.

"She lives in a cabin behind it. I think she rents it from the woman who owns the white house. Occasionally, I'd see her at Mass, but I haven't seen her in a while. The last time I spoke to my friend, I inquired about her. He told me, as far as he knew, she still lived there. But that was about three months ago."

Mother leaned forward a little more and looked at Father Tom. "Oh?" she said.

"At one point, I understand, she was preparing to become a nun. My friend told me she made her temporary vows, but then just before it was time for her make her final vows, she decided against the religious life. Apparently, she came to realize she wasn't one for a vocation in the church.

"My friend said he was quite impressed with her and her work with natural remedies. Do you know about homeopathy?"

"I've heard of it," Mother said. "Jack has said some good things about it."

Father Tom continued. "Apparently, those who couldn't find help from traditional medicine have sought her help for various illnesses and she's had some good success. I understand that the way to see her is through a recommendation."

Father Tom gave Mother a serious look. He clasped his hands and placed them under his chin. He twitched his mouth as if he wanted to say more but stopped.

"What else do you know about her?" Mother asked.

"Well, my friend referred to her approach as holistic. He said her methods are based on balancing the mind and the body."

Father Tom coughed several times. The phlegm rattled around in the back of his throat. It was a deep cough, the kind that came from way down in the bottom of the chest. Mother said he used to smoke cigarettes before he switched to cigars to lessen the effect on his lungs.

I watched a squirrel climb the branches on the tree outside, darting in and out among the leaves that remained, and hummed a little tune—one that I'd made up.

"If you want to see her, I can try to set up a meeting." Father said.

Mother turned away from Father Tom and looked at me sitting in my chair. It was the same look I had seen many times before: a sad, forlorn kind of look. A "something is really wrong with you and I have no idea what to do about it," kind of look. She adjusted her legs in the chair and sat straight up.

"Father, can I talk to you alone in your office please?"

Mother and the priest stood up. Father Tom glanced at the cigar smoldering in the ash tray, but didn't pick it up. Instead, he ushered my mother into his office and closed the door. I tip-toed over and listened to them through the cracks. I heard them whispering.

"If you think this woman can help, I want to go see her. But you have to tell me more about her."

There was a long silence. I got ready to tip-toe back to my chair, but I heard them whispering again.

"I don't know much more about her, only that she's apparently quite gifted and she's had some good success. I knew when I first met her, she was a free spirit. There was something special about her. Something I couldn't quite put my finger on—something mystical. My priest friend told me that as she became more and more involved in the healing work she decided to leave the religious life. These things happen. She left of her own free will. That's really all I know."

I heard the sound of a chair scraping against the floor. Then Mother's voice again. "Why do you think I should go to her?"

"Carmela, the boy's been struggling for a few years now with these dreams. Clearly something is going on with him, and perhaps it's beyond our abilities to help him. I've been praying for him. Maybe it's the work of the Lord. Maybe it's something else. I just don't know. But perhaps this woman can help him."

"What do you mean by 'the work of the Lord,' Father?"

"I mean that he may have special gifts and abilities. It may be that he is being called to a vocation. But I just don't know. It could also mean that dark forces are battling for him as well."

I heard a gasp.

"Father, are you serious? Do you really believe that—about the dark forces?"

"Carmela, there are things that happen to people that we don't completely understand. I know you know about these kinds of things—the dark night of the soul and so on. I believe he's young for that, but it may be something similar. That may be what's going on with the dreams. But we must be careful about subscribing any of this to God or otherwise.

"It may be that Joey is just under some kind of emotional stress. But I don't think it's anything for us to get too carried away with just yet. He's still a young boy. Why not take him to see this woman, and see what happens. Perhaps she'll be able to tell you what's going on. I know this much about her: She's a person of goodness and love. That was clear to me the first time I met her. So it won't hurt him to see her, and it might help."

And then neither of them said anything for a while. I heard a chair squeak. I heard a sound like the shuffling of papers. I heard Father clear his throat again. I heard a long, drawn-out sigh that could only have come from my mother.

"If you want me to try to set up a meeting with her, I'll see what I can do. But it's up to you. It's your decision."

It was quiet for a little while. Then another sigh.

"Okay, okay...if she was preparing to be a nun she must be a good person. Go ahead and set it up Father."

I heard them walking across the room. I scurried back to my chair. The door opened and Mother and the priest walked back in.

"Oh, one more thing," Father said, as he ushered Mother toward me. "The woman's name is Ava. Please try not to worry about Joey." He glanced at me and smiled. "He's going to be just fine."

Mother knelt and touched my shoulder. Tears threatened to fall from her eyes again. "Joey, you've been such a good boy today," she said. "I'm going to take you to get some ice-cream."

Mother looked at Father Tom. "Thank you so much for your time today, Father," she said.

Father Tom nodded and said, "Oh, not at all. Let me know how things go, okay?"

Mother reached for my hand and together we walked outside. There was still plenty of daylight left for play, and Paddy jumped and ran in circles when he saw me.

MEETING AVA

I knew her only as Ava.

It took nearly a month for the priest to set up the meeting. Mother waited impatiently, until finally, one morning, about two weeks before Thanksgiving, she got the call. The next morning we drove the winding country road that led to Ava's house. As instructed, Mother parked the car in the vacant lot across the street from the two-storey white house with the black shutters. We knocked on the door and were greeted by a short, pleasant, middle-aged woman, with teased black hair.

"Oh no, I'm not Ava. I'm Martha," she chuckled, after we asked. "Ava lives down by the river. Just follow the trail over there. She's expecting you." She pointed to an opening in the woods. "Just follow the stone trail until you come to the end. Right there, where the trail ends and makes a 'Y' you go left on the dirt path, and you keep on walking and before long you'll come to another 'Y' and you go right. After that you'll see her house. Be careful now, the stones can get slippery this time of year." We headed down the trail, following a path of gray stones of close to the same size, with some differences in coloring. Some were speckled with silver, like granite; others were nearly black. But they made the trail easy to follow.

As Mother and I approached the second 'Y,' I noticed a circle carved into the bark of an oak tree whose roots had grown into the trail, causing the stones to jut at weird angles. Just past the tree, in the clearing, there was a cabin made of the same gray stone we had followed on the trail. Next to the cabin stood a greenhouse made of wood planks, with lots of windows on one side and on the top of one section of its roof.

The sun had just risen above the trees, casting a lemon yellow hue on the trees' barren limbs. The cabin's walnut-colored door was closed. Mother held my hand and knocked on the door. There was no answer. She knocked again. I heard something behind me and turned around. A tall woman with auburn hair pulled back loosely in a ponytail walked towards us carrying a wicker basket full of dried flowers, herbs and twigs. Some of the flowers had strayed from her basket, and clung to the front of her sky-blue turtleneck.

"Hello," she said.

Mother turned, and let go of my hand. She walked toward the woman. "Hello. I'm Carmela, and this is my son, Joey. Are you Ava?"

The woman answered in a voice that was quiet and yet strong. "Yes, I'm Ava."

"Nice to meet you," Mother said. She reached toward Ava, offering a handshake, but Ava didn't notice, or pretended not to.

"Please come inside," Ava said. The woman shifted her gaze to me and looked deeply into my eyes.

I looked away. This woman knows all about me, I thought. She knows about my dreams. She knows about my secret. Something about the way she looked at me with her self-assured, half-smile, made me feel I knew her too. She looked a lot like the woman in my dreams. She touched my shoulder to guide me toward the door. As we walked into the cabin, Mother fumbled around with her purse. She fussed with her hair, pressing and patting at the already neatly groomed strands. "Thank you so much for seeing us," Mother said. "I can't tell you how much this means to me. I've heard such good things about you…"

"Please sit down," the woman said. "I know why you're here. Father Tom told me about Joey. I know what's going on with him. I know about his dreams and premonitions."

The woman pulled two chairs away from a rectangular wooden table, one for Mother and one for me. She smiled ever so slightly as she turned and pulled out a third chair. She motioned toward the chairs indicating again that we should sit down.

I looked around the room as Mother and Ava talked. Creamy-white plaster walls framed the room. The floor was made of ochre-colored tiles and was partially covered by green and red and brown braided rugs. Except for a few tables with candles on them, the room was uncluttered and neat. A simple, carved, wooden rose with five petals hung on the wall above an entry-way to another room. Sheer ivory-colored curtains draping to the floor made it difficult for me to see in.

"We have a lot to talk about," Ava said. "Would you like something warm to drink? Tea or coffee? I could make some hot chocolate, or…

Hot chocolate! Did someone say hot chocolate? I jumped on the chance. "I'll have some hot choc…"

"Joey!" Mother exclaimed. She turned to Ava apologetically. "Sorry, it's his favorite treat."

"I'll be happy to make some for him," Ava said. She smiled at me as if we were long lost friends. And, strangely, that's how it felt.

"Thank you, that's kind of you." Mother gave me a stern look. "Yes, some tea would be nice," she said, still eyeing me.

Ava whisked around the kitchen and placed a pot and a kettle on the stove. She turned and looked at me. "So you're having some scary dreams," she said. "I want to talk to you about that, but first I want to talk to your mother—okay?"

I nodded my head.

My mind wandered away from the conversation. I heard them talking in the background but my attention was drawn to the room on the other side of the curtains.

Ava returned to the table. She and Mother talked and I listened and after a while I got bored and asked if I could go look in the other room. Mother looked at Ava. Ava hesitated, and then she said, of course, and Mother told me not to touch anything, and that was that, and off I went.

I parted the curtains and walked into the room. The room was bright and airy and it seemed familiar to me, as if I belonged there, as if I had returned home from a long vacation. In one corner, a group of white candles on a wooden table flickered in the morning light. In another corner, a stream of incense smoke drifted toward the ceiling in a straight line, until it was interrupted by a draft of air. The room smelled of cedar and pine.

Peacock feathers were arranged in vases scattered about the room: iridescent green with blue and bronze colored eyes. Bright colored shawls with intricate patterns lay draped over chairs.

A deck of cards was positioned on yet another wooden table. The top card was a picture of a young man with long golden hair riding a steed and holding a spear. Behind the young man, a white sun in an amber sky formed a halo around his head. The man on the horse looked like Jesus. On the bottom of the card were the words: The Sun.

Crystals of various shapes rested on other tables and bookcases; a chiseled stone cross hung on a wall near one of the windows. I picked up a blue and white bowl with little yellow stars inside and spun it around a few times. I heard Mother and Ava talking and remembered that Mother told me not to touch anything, so I set the bowl on the table and walked towards a funny looking picture on one of the walls. As I moved away from the table, I bumped it hard with my leg. The table shook and the bowl fell to the floor, but didn't break. Mother called, "Joey! Please be careful. I told you not to touch. Please come back in here now."

I heard Mother speaking to Ava. "I'm so sorry," she said, "He likes to pick things up. He knows better. I'm trying to teach him not to touch things that don't belong to him."

"It's okay," Ava said, "Let the boy explore. He's interested in what he sees. That's a good sign."

"He needs to come back and sit down. Joey, come have your hot chocolate."

I walked back and sat down. Ava had placed a cup of hot chocolate on the table for me. It smelled of cocoa, cinnamon, and vanilla. "Here you go," Ava said, "a delicious, natural remedy. Did you know the Mayans and the Aztecs used chocolate two thousand years ago? It wasn't sweet, though, the way we drink it today. And it didn't contain milk — dairy animals didn't come to the New World until the Spaniards did. But all in all, it's good for the tummy, and many other things, if you know the secret recipe." Ava smiled.

Mother tilted her head. "Really? I had no idea."

Ava placed two cups of tea on the table: one for Mother and one for herself, and a plate of cookies for all of us. I reached for a cookie and looked at Mother. She nodded her head in approval. "Okay, but just one," she said. Mother looked back at Ava. "I'm sorry. Did you ask me a question? I can't remember what we were talking about…"

"That's quite all right. What did Father Tom tell you about me?"

"Oh yes, he told me that you are a gifted woman," Mother said. "He told me you've had some good success with natural remedies."

"What did he say about that?" Ava asked.

Ava slid her cup around the table waiting for Mother's response.

"Well, not much more. Only that you've had good success and that you might be able to help Joey with his nightmares."

Ava tugged at her turtleneck sweater. She smiled. "I think I might be able to help him," she said. "I've had some experience working with dreams. It's just a matter of finding the right remedy to bring him back into balance. It shouldn't be too difficult."

Mother swallowed hard. "That would be such a blessing."

Ava sat back and folded her arms across her chest.

"Is there anything else you want to know about me?"

Mother wrung her hands and looked around the room.

"Well, one last thing. Father Tom told me that you were preparing to be a nun but you changed your mind."

Ava took a sip from her cup and set it down on the table. "Yes, at one time I wanted to be a nun. I spent a number of years living in a religious community. It was a meaningful time for me. But ultimately, I realized the Lord had other plans for me. I decided to dedicate my life to the study of natural healing and to serve the Lord by helping people in that way."

Mother tilted her head slightly and smiled. "That's very nice. I'm sure it was a hard choice."

"Oh, not so hard," Ava said.

Mother picked up her tea cup and looked into it. She didn't drink.

"You know, my husband Jack is a physician," Mother said.

"I know, Father Tom told me," Ava replied. "How does he feel about you being here?"

"He's not as concerned about Joey as I am. I haven't told him much about you and he hasn't asked. He trusts me to do what I need to do. He thinks I'm being overprotective and that Joey is just going through a phase.

He's a busy man. I take care of our boys and my husband works. That's the way we live. He's a good father. He tries to spend time with Joey and the other boys, and when he does, it's a good time with them. But he's busy providing for our family and his focus is on his work."

Ava watched me closely. But she did it in a way that Mother didn't notice. I noticed. I saw her watching. But it didn't bother me.

Mother reached across the table and placed her hand on Ava's arm. Ava flinched a bit, but didn't pull away. Mother looked at Ava. "Look, I know you're doing us a favor. I know we wouldn't be here if it wasn't for Father Tom. I'm going to trust you with my son. Please take good care of him. He's precious to me."

Ava nodded and said, "I know."

Mother glanced at me. Her eyes were watery. She reached for my hand and turned toward Ava. "I hope you can help us," Mother said.

"You can trust me," Ava said. "I can already see that Joey's quite perceptive. I'd like to spend some time with him and see if I can help him with his nightmares. Let's just take this one step at a time, okay."

Mother nodded agreement.

Ava stood and began to gather the cups from the table. "Things will get clearer in a little while. We can get started right away—next weekend if you can manage. You'll need to have him here maybe once a month for awhile until I am able to get him in balance. Once I get him balanced we won't need to meet as often. Can you manage that?"

"I can manage," Mother said.

"Okay then, we'll set it up for next weekend. Do you mind if I have a few minutes alone with Joey now?" Ava asked.

Mother looked at me. I could see she was thinking about whether or not she would allow this. But then she said, "No, not at all. I'll just step outside for a while."

Mother walked to the door, opened it, and walked outside. Ava motioned for me to come closer, and she reached for my hand.

"Do you understand what your mother and I are talking about?"

"Yes, I think so." I said. I looked at Ava. She reached into one of her pockets and pulled out a silver disc, the size of a quarter. On one side it had roses like the roses that ran along the fence in the front of our yard. On the other side it had a circle with a dot in the center that looked like the ring of smoke from my dream.

Ava smiled. She held the disc over her heart for a moment, and then she handed it to me. "Here, I'd like you to have this," she said.

THE SNOW CAVE

My head jerks and I wake up coughing and gasping for breath. It's dark again. I'm cold. So cold. I try to move and then I remember the pain in my legs.

My whole body hurts now. Every bone aches. The peace and calm of the cottage, the woman in the rose dress, the little boy, the pastel light and colors from my dream—if it was a dream—are faint, but comforting memories. So I try to hold on to them. I try to go back. I try to fall asleep again, hoping I can get back there. But I can't.

I try to pull myself up, slowly, gently, ever so slightly, to avoid the pain. When I move, particles of ice and snow bounce off my head and face. I cry. Somebody help me please. Tears flow down my cheeks. Hot, wet, salty water dribbles slowly into the corners of my mouth.

It's so cold. And I'm afraid in the blackness, and the loneliness, and the despair, and the thoughts of death. I weep. I cry out for help. On and on, until finally, I exhaust myself.

Then out of nowhere, I hear a sound. I know that voice.

"Give me your hand," the voice says.

I lift my hand high above my head grasping for something, anything. But I feel nothing. Yet I reach out, up into the darkness. But still, there's nothing.

"Don't give up!"

"Albert, is that you? Help me!"

I stretch even more. Then I feel fingers on mine and a small hand on my hand, and then two small hands reach in and grab my arms and pull me up out of the cave. And suddenly its morning and springtime and the sun is shining and birds are chirping and I'm standing in a field of tall green grass.

"How did you find me?"

"I heard you calling out. Come on, let's go!"

The boy stands for a moment and then turns and runs. Is it Albert? If it is, he's a teenage boy: thirteen or fourteen. I run after him.

"Where are we going?"

"To the river, Paul's waiting for us," he says.

Yes, of course, the river. I stop for a moment and look behind me for the hole in the ground and the snow. It's not there.

"Albert, it is you. Wait up!"

The boy stops, turns, and runs back to me.

"What's the matter?" he asks, "We have to hurry. Paul's waiting for us."

"But what about the man trapped in the snow, what happened to him?" I ask.

Albert blinks his eyes. He tugs on his dungarees to pull them up over his hips. "He's dying," he says. "Don't worry about him anymore. Come on, let's go!" He turns and runs again through the tall green grass.

We run as fast as we can past the old shamrock tree, past the three barking dogs in their kennels, over the crooked ditch, past the two shanties. The yellow sun blazes in the sky. We run and run. I reach forward to touch the boy in front of me, but he moves too fast.

I feel the sun on my face, the warmth on my skin, and it feels so good. We run until we reach the river. As we approach, I see another boy kneeling on the ground. When he sees us coming, he waves his hand high in the air.

"Come quick!" he yells. "It's almost ready to launch."

It's Paul. He's building the raft. He kneels on the ground and wraps a long twisted rope around an old whiskey barrel, underneath its planks of wood which are held together with rusty nails and hinges. He pulls the rope tight and asks me to hold the barrel in place while he ties the rope off with a sailor's knot. "The barrels will make it float," Paul says. "There, that should do it. Let's push it into the water."

We bend together close to the ground and push until the raft slides from the grassy river bank into a shallow cove away from the flowing current of the murky brown water. Albert takes his shoes off and rolls his pants above his knees. He steps into the water and holds onto the raft with one hand.

"It's cold!" he says, as he wades further into the water.

Paul stands with his hands on his hips as he watches the raft bob up and down. "Look, it works. It floats!" Paul says.

The wooden planks of the raft bob on the water, buoyed by the four barrels. Albert climbs onto the raft, kneels and grabs a rope tied to the front of it. "Okay, now push me into the river." Albert says.

I stop and look at the sky, at the puffy white clouds. They're floating like great dollops of whipped cream in a gigantic blueberry milkshake. I remember this day. Then suddenly for a brief moment I remember something else — I remember being trapped in the snow and ice. I realize I'm half-remembering — half-hallucinating. And for a moment, just a brief, tiny moment, I'm back in the snow cave. And then — just as fast, I'm back on the river bank.

I push the raft into the flowing water. And the sun is warm on my face. And we're together — Paul and Albert and me — all together again. And for a little while it all feels so real and so good. So I push, and the raft floats out into the middle of the river with Albert kneeling and laughing and yelling at the tops of his lungs and pumping his fist and raising a paddle high above his head. "Yes! Yes! It floats. Whoa! Watch me go."

I feel the pain in my legs and for a brief moment the sky is getting dark and it's almost night time and I know I'll have to go back to the snow cave soon.

Paul stands on the river bank and waves to Albert out in the middle of the river. Then he looks at me. "What's the matter Joe?" he says.

I snap back from the darkness and I'm on the river bank again and the sun is shining. "I'm just taking it all in — that's all — it's such a beautiful day — I'd forgotten how much fun we had together."

Paul opens his mouth and raises an eyebrow and looks at me. I know he doesn't understand. How could he? I don't understand either. All I know is I won't be with him and Albert by the river much longer. But I don't let on that I know. I play along because it feels so good and so free and I don't want to go back to the cave. I don't want to feel the pain and the cold. I don't want to lie there freezing in the dark. I don't want to be afraid anymore. And most of all, I don't want to die.

The raft floats along in the river current. I remember this day now. I've lived it. The raft will float slowly until it reaches the merge point, the spot where the faster water from the other side of the low ridge joins it. It will pick up speed and enter the dangerous rapids that lead to Sugar Falls.

Once it gets past the merge point, it'll be too late. We've played down by the river in the springtime many times before and we know the danger of the fast waters that lead to Sugar Falls. It's a long way to the falls from the merge point, but at that point, the rapids move fast and furious and it will be too late for Albert to recover.

Sugar Falls drops nearly thirty feet onto jagged rocks and ledges. An unlucky man rode a canoe over the falls a few years back; they found his body and pieces of his canoe in the lake a week later. When we were kids we'd shoot our pellet guns at empty paint cans we tied to the trees and floated in the water below the falls. The cans were perfect targets for us as we learned to shoot the pellet guns we all got on the same long-past Christmas morning.

Today Paul has a plan. Albert gets the first ride on the raft because he's the oldest. Long before Albert gets to the merge point, he's going to paddle the raft over to the side of the river bank, to the place where we built our fort, and toss a rope to Paul and me. We'll pull him over to the side, and he'll get out and we'll celebrate our first attempt at sailing a raft on the river. That's the plan. But that's not what happens. On this day, just at the point where Albert begins to paddle to the side of the river, something unexpected happens.

"Okay Albert! Start paddling this way!" Paul yells.

Paul and I run along the bank of the river and follow the raft, and Albert.

"Meet me at the fort!" Albert yells.

Paul jumps into the air, pumps his clenched fist several times, looks up and yells into the sky, "Look at him go!"

The river flows fast and carries the raft along as small ripples of white water appear. This is well beyond the spot where Albert is supposed to begin paddling to the fort. But he's having fun. He's caught up in the excitement.

Suddenly, one of the planks cracks and a whiskey barrel breaks away. "Albert—the raft—it's coming apart!" Paul yells.

The raft splits in two. Albert tries to move onto the larger of the two parts. His foot slips. He falls into the water. He's under for a long time. He comes up gasping. The current pulls him down. We see his head above the water. We yell, "Grab the barrel!" He reaches for it, goes under, and comes up again. We see his arms wrapped around the barrel. But he is close, too close, to the merge point.

"We have to help him Joe!" Paul yells.

Albert rolls in the water, arms clutching the barrel, but the barrel is slick and smooth and hard for him to hold on to. He's grasping at it, trying to use it to float. Just beyond the merge point, far ahead of us, he'll have only one chance to grab a large tree branch hanging from the other side of the riverbank just a few inches above the water, almost in the middle of the river. The branch has been hanging over the water for almost a year. We couldn't get to the other side to see how it fell, but we told ourselves it was probably hit by lightening.

Albert streams along, bouncing up and down in the water. He sees the branch coming. He raises a hand and tries to hold on to the barrel with the other. The branch is coming up fast, and quickly he's under it. He lunges for it, and he has it. The branch bends and cracks, but it holds him. The barrel slips away and tumbles toward Sugar Falls.

"He did it! He grabbed the branch!" Paul yells.

Albert holds onto the branch with both hands. He breathes fast. It's not possible for him to swim to us because the current is too fast and he doesn't have the strength left. But when he tries to pull himself further up the branch, it sags into the water. He's stuck. If he doesn't hold on, the current will take him over the falls. The branch is cracked and slowly splintering. We have to do something to help him.

I know exactly what to do. We keep an old inner tube with a rope tied to it on a tree near the merge point. I'll run get it, and throw it to Albert, and we'll pull him in. I see it clearly. The only problem is, for my idea to work, Albert will have to let go of the branch.

"Paul, meet me at the point. I'll grab the tube. Tell Albert I'm on my way!" I run to the tree as fast as I can, untie the tube, and run to the merge point. When I get there, Paul is standing on the riverbank yelling to Albert, telling him I'm on my way.

I heave the tube into the water but it doesn't make it far enough for Albert to reach. I pull the tube back and try throwing it again. It still doesn't make it. The only way it's going to work is for Albert to let go of the branch and swim. "When I throw the tube, let go of the branch and swim to it!" I yell.

Paul kneels on the ground, cups his hands around his mouth and yells, "Let go Albert—let go and swim to the tube!"

Albert tries to pull himself up out of the water and further up the branch, but the branch cracks even more.

I yell, "No, don't pull the branch—it's going to break!"

Albert is scared. He's cold and I know he's tired. I look at Paul. I have another idea. If Paul can tie the inner tube rope around a tree, I can swim the inner tube out to Albert, and try to coax him to let go of the branch and swim to me. When I have him, Paul will pull us in. It's our only chance. I tell Paul the plan. "I'm a better swimmer than you, but you're stronger," I say. "If I can get to him, you can pull us in." Paul agrees. He ties off the rope quickly and within seconds I'm in the cold water swimming with the current, toward Albert.

When I get close enough, I yell at Albert to let go. But he's scared and he's holding on tight to the branch.

"You have to let go and swim to me Albert—the branch is going to break!"

Albert doesn't listen, or maybe he can't hear me. He lunges at the branch, but the counter-movement pushes him under the surface. The branch is going to break at any moment.

"Albert, let go of the branch—swim to me—grab my hand!"

"I can't! I can't! I won't make it to you," he wails.

Water splashes in my eyes and gushes into my mouth. I spit it out. I'm within a few yards of Albert's outstretched hand. "You can do it Albert—just let go, I'll grab your hand."

"No, no—I can't!" He begins to cry: big wrenching sobs of fear and frustration.

"You have to let go. The branch is going to break."

Paul stands on the riverbank, holding the stretched rope, ready to pull us to the shore. "Let go Albert! Let go!" he yells.

~

And then I'm in the snow cave again. It's dark and cold and I hear Paul's words, but the words are softer now, muted and gentle. "Let go—Let go," Paul says. And I realize it's me that needs to let go. I'm hallucinating and I'm dying. I'm between life and death and memories and dreams.

There's a part of me that wants to be rid of the pain and the cold and the suffering—the part of me that wants to die. And there's a part of me that wants to hold on, and that's the part of me that clings to life, the part of me that wants to live. And I see it all so clearly: the enormous struggle between holding on and letting go. I see how I held on to things in my life that no longer served me even when I knew it was time to move on.

I see how I held on to what was safe and comfortable rather than letting go and following my heart. And in this moment I know. But how can I let go now. What will that mean? Will I die? Or will a part of me that no longer serves me die? I don't know. I'm just like Albert in the river, clinging desperately to what I think is safe.

I hear the words again. "Let go! Let go!" And slowly the darkness fades and it's bright again and I'm back in the river splashing and reaching for Albert's hand and begging him to let go of the branch.

Albert tries one more time to pull himself up. He lunges upward in a desperate attempt to climb the branch to safety. There's a loud snap. The branch breaks with Albert clinging to it, and Albert and the branch begin to float away.

"Let go Albert!" I scream.

Albert lets go and lunges toward me. His sinks below the water and thrashes his arms and legs in a desperate attempt to reach me. I feel his fingers scratching my hand. I feel his fingers on my forearm and I grab his arm and pull him toward me. He wraps his arms around my neck and his legs around my back. Paul sees him and he pulls on the rope using those big strong hands and arms, and brings us in.

When we get to the edge, Paul drags us onto the wet ground. Albert and I flop onto our backs and gulp air. Paul sits and looks at us. Then he looks at his hands, red and raw from rope burns. The sun is warm on my face as I lie on the ground, my chest pounding for breath.

But once again the scene begins to fade.

"Wait, where are you going?" Paul asks, as he tips his head to one side. "Stay here with us."

"Can't you stay just a little longer, Joe?" Albert asks.

But my time is up. The blackness sets in again and Albert and Paul and the river are gone. I'm back in the snow cave, in the darkness, with the pain and the terror, shivering and shaking, desperately and tenuously holding on to my life. And then, almost effortlessly, I drift into the other dream, or the unconsciousness, or whatever it is that's keeping me alive.

1960

Ava was sad that day. I saw it in the way she smiled; the way she tilted her head and held her lips together, barely moving the corners of her mouth upwards in the semblance of a smile. The lines around her mouth ran in shallow crevices to her chin, threatening to hold her face in contempt at any sign of joy. She had aged in the five years since our first meeting.

On that day, as on many other occasions, we walked the path of herb-strewn stones that lead to the greenhouse just a short distance from her cabin. When we went in, as usual, I pulled my spiral-bound sketch book from my book bag and placed it on the table.

What was it? What had her so absorbed? Maybe she'd had a dream: a dispatch from another dimension, a bulletin from a hidden realm. She'd called them all of these things, over time. She was prone to these sudden revelations, she said. Part of her curse, she said. She made light of it sometimes when she was happy. And yet, she told me they were serious and precise when they came: these visions.

Some brought warnings of illness or misfortune; others brought promise of new beginnings or goodwill. But when they brought a message of certain death or impending doom to someone she loved, she mourned. And the sadness showed. She couldn't conceal it. That much I had learned as she intensified her teachings during the previous six months.

She knew she could do nothing about the foreboding message when it came. The event could not be altered, the outcome could not be changed, the consequence had been established. It will be as it must be, she said. She could only take the insight into her soul and harbor it. She sat on it, the way the robin on the rose trellis sat on her chicks, guarding the fledglings from the gray striped cat who lurked underneath.

That day she told me she would teach me more about the significance of dreams and premonitions, and later, about the flow of time. That was her real gift, she said. When her insights began, she no longer talked much about her healing remedies. Now, except for a few varieties of medicinal herbs, vegetables and flowers took up most of the space in the glass room.

For the last year she had been intrigued, almost obsessed, with the study of symbols, and patterns. I had seen some of them spread out on her table in an assortment of colored papers and ink. Sacred geometry, she called it. The symbols are thought by some to open a portal, she said. They are beings that can balance thoughts and emotions and bring clear seeing and deep understanding.

She referred to them as beings. I wasn't entirely sure what she meant by that. She told me these symbols had come to her in a dream years before. And then she had had a fateful meeting with a sage who explained their significance just before he died. She associated the symbols with holiness and inspiration. Grace.

She'd been working with three symbols in a certain sequence. And there was a fourth, she said, the one she had been told could enable her to alter the future, and enable her to access the hidden powers of the universe, the one that would reveal the secret of immortality. She spoke of a new world of heightened awareness and the peak evolution of the human form. This was what she had been waiting for.

She said I might have some information that would lead her to the fourth symbol. Was she talking about my dreams again? I thought we had moved past all of that stuff several years ago. But I was curious. I asked her several times to tell me about the three symbols, or better yet, show me. She didn't think I was ready.

On this particular day, though, she hinted that if we completed our lesson with time to spare before Mother came, she might show me the first symbol.

~

Ava had long before determined that she would pass on the knowledge of the symbols to me. She decided this as we neared the end of our first year together. In one particular lesson, she placed a clear stone, a piece of jewelry that looked like a beetle, and a statue of St. Joseph in front of me, and asked me to make a story. I don't remember the story I made, for I was only eight then. The story satisfied her.

After that, she explained the meaning of the carved, wooden rose above the entry-way door.

"It means that some things are special secrets between people," she said. "From now on some of the things I'm going to show you will be our secret. You will remember that won't you?"

I nodded yes. I agreed to keep her teachings secret. Now, I was becoming a man, Ava said, and it was almost time.

But sometimes her words confused me. I didn't know what she meant when she talked about a new world, or heightened awareness, or peak evolution. I did notice she had become more peaceful and less rigid and strict since she started working with the symbols.

She lit a candle. She placed it on a small table in the room with the glass roof, the room that let the sunlight in year-round, the room where flowers grew. I sat in a creaky wooden chair next to the table. Ava stood, closing the last of the books that were spread out before us.

"You have progressed well, young man," she said. "You're coming into balance quite nicely." She spun around, almost allowing herself to smile, almost allowing herself to feel happy.

"Are you going to show me the symbols today?" I asked.

Ava looked up through the glass in the ceiling. A grayish-white bird drifted above the trees. She squinted and shaded her eyes with her hand. "That's unusual," she said, "A seagull so far from the lake."

I looked up and saw the bird fluttering in the breeze.

The bird dipped toward the glass roof of the greenhouse.

"No, it's not a gull, it's a dove!" Ava exclaimed, "A white dove. That's a good omen. Yes, I believe you are ready for the first symbol. It will bring good luck."

She saw the bird as a sign. She'd been looking for signs: something to convince her that it was time to let me in. But I had become unsure of her self-proclaimed alchemy and clairvoyance. Slowly, over the past year, I'd become skeptical of her tutoring.

My nightmares and premonitions were a distant memory, gone away, thankfully, after the first few sessions Ava and I had together. Now, I was more interested in playing baseball and in girls.

"Well" I said. "What about the first symbol? You said you would show me if we finished in time. Well?"

Ava returned her attention to me. "I'll give you a hint," she said "Do you remember your dreams of the angel?"

I turned away and trailed my finger across the table. "Yes."

Ava took a few steps toward me so she could look directly at my face. "Do you remember the dream when she showed you the image?"

That seemed so long ago. It seemed to me that the dreams had happened in another lifetime, to someone else, not me. But when she asked me the question, the memories came rushing in, and I remembered the dream of the woman I used to refer to as an angel. I hadn't thought about that since Ava and I first met. "Yes, I remember," I said. "It was a circle, or a ring, with something in the center of it."

"Ah, you remember!" she said. She held up her finger. "Just a moment."

She walked into a darkened room. I followed her and stood just outside the doorway. She opened a drawer in a brown wooden chest and pulled out an ivory colored packet. She motioned to me: Come in.

Ava opened the packet and pulled out a piece of thick, white paper. It was similar in size to a page from my sketch book. A stark black symbol dominated the white page: A bold black ring encircled a single black dot.

She held the paper in her hands, thumbs on top and fingers underneath. She lifted the paper before her eyes for a moment then placed it on the table before me. "Pick it up. Look at it," she said.

I held the paper just as she had: thumbs on top, fingers underneath. I raised the paper to eye level, and gazed into it. I was drawn into its center, into its boldness, into its elegant design.

"What do you see?" she asked.

How could I answer that question? I didn't know what I saw. I didn't know what I felt. "It looks like an eye," I said, "An eye looking into my eyes."

Ava nodded. I saw her, but I didn't want to shift my focus away from the symbol.

"Do you see the light?" Ava asked.

I wasn't sure—then yes, I saw a shimmer of light around the edges of the ring.

"Do you see the light," Ava asked again.

"Yes."

"Where is it?" she asked.

"Around the circle," I answered.

Ava placed her hand on my shoulder. And as she spoke, she seemed to choose her words carefully, speaking also to something beyond me.

"What does it mean?" I asked.

"We don't necessarily assign a meaning to it," she said. "But when I look at this symbol I feel that the center represents my heart's core — my true path. And I know if I listen and follow that path I will be protected. And that's what the outer ring represents to me — God's protection.

"This is an ancient symbol," she said. "Some believe it originated in Egypt, long ago. At some point, a Greek mathematician named Pythagoras discovered it. Later he discovered other symbols. He discovered the power they possessed when he meditated on them in a certain sequence. He realized the symbols could help him access insights and unique abilities. He passed the knowledge on to some of his students. It came to be considered dangerous knowledge during the Dark Ages and was hidden for centuries."

Ava took the symbol away from me.

The image remained in the air in front of me…just like…just like it did with…the angel. It was the image from the dream. I tried to touch the image as it floated in the air, closed my eyes and saw it again, but when I opened my eyes it was gone.

Ava stood still.

~

In earlier lessons Ava had taught me how to meditate: first by just sitting quietly and focusing on my breath to quiet my mind. She taught me how to listen to my inner voice. Then she taught me how to use a mantra, a special sound, a combination of syllables, first aloud and then silently, in the stillness. She had spoken of special outward symbols, which she said could increase one's vibration and create greater balance and harmony. Was this one of them?

She gave me instructions. She taught me how to use the symbol to center myself. She told me about the power of the light around the edges. "It is pure," she said.

When we finished it was nearly dark outside. Something about Ava had changed. "Your mother will be waiting," she said. "Be easy on yourself over the next few weeks. If you have the fire dream you must tell me." She said it again. "You must tell me. It is very important for you to remember this. If you have any disturbing dreams, you must tell me. Do you understand?"

I nodded.

Ava slid the symbol into the ivory packet. She placed it between the pages of my sketch book. "Put it in your book bag for now," she said. "When you get home, find a special place for it."

"Is this one of our secrets?" I asked.

Ava smiled. "You've learned well," she said.

I stared at Ava then looked down at the table. "Okay," I said.

Ava looked back at me. She was quiet. Then she turned and walked to the door. "It's getting late. Your mother will be waiting for you."

∼

I followed Ava's instructions. Or so I thought. I found a place for the symbol: in my bedroom closet, underneath the stacks of books and boxes of old clothes that hadn't been touched in years, a place no one would think or care to look. I followed her instructions about how to use the symbol: how long and how often to look at it. And just as she said, I began to experience a greater sense of calm and confidence.

During that first week, I moved through my days with ease. My family and friends commented on the change in me. You seem happier, they said, and more relaxed. They wanted to know what was going on. But I didn't say anything about the symbol. I kept it to myself.

At night, I dreamed vivid dreams: I dreamed of walking through fields of magnificent red and yellow and orange wild-flowers by the lake. I dreamed of floating with purple balloon-like orbs, mingling with the clouds. I dreamed of peaceful things—gentle waterfalls, fresh fallen snow early in the morning with no footprints. These dreams comforted me and filled my nights of restful sleep.

If I felt like this after using just the first symbol, what would it be like to have the other two, I thought. I couldn't wait to tell Ava that I was ready to see them, as soon as she was ready to show me. And although I remembered Ava's warning about disturbing dreams, as time went by and I had none, I thought less frequently about what she had said to me.

And then one night, like a bolt of lightning in a darkened sky, I dreamed of the fire again. Just like the dream I had when I was a child. And in my dream, orange flames and black smoke billowed into the dark night sky. In this dream, my house was destroyed with my family in it. I seemed to be watching from far away.

Yet, strangely, I awakened in the early hours of the day feeling peaceful. For a while, I stared at the yellow moonlight seeping through the curtains of my window. Then I drifted back to sleep.

In the morning, I thought that I should ride my bike to Ava's house after school, and tell her about the dream. But my afternoons were filled with activities. I was on the football team, I was president of the math club, and sometimes Mother had chores for me. The days slipped by.

Every evening I told myself that I would make time to get in touch with Ava the next day, but something else always seemed more pressing. After awhile, the dream and the promise I made to Ava became nothing more than a subtle tug on my sleeve that I eventually decided to disregard. And after all, I rationalized, the dream hadn't upset me as it had when I was a child.

But deep down, I knew I hadn't followed Ava's instructions.

Albert's sixteenth birthday came a few days later. Weeks before, I had told my mother that Albert would love it if Paul and I could spend the birthday night at Albert's house. So Aunt Leah, Albert's mother, invited Paul and me to spend the night over as part of the party.

I was in the basement messing around with my father's lantern when my mother opened the door to call down the stairs, "Joey! You better get over there now."

As I ran out the door, my mother cautioned me to stay away from the river. It was full and swift after the recent spring rains. I ran past a cleared lot where a hole for the foundation of a new home had been dug. I stopped and picked up a rock and threw it into the hole. Then I started running again. And on my way to Albert's house that feeling of forgetfulness tugged at my sleeve again. Had I forgotten to do something?

～

As Aunt Leah prepared the birthday dinner, the three of us headed to the field next to Albert's house. At first, we only intended to throw the baseball around. But soon, Albert got bored.

"Hey, let's go to the river," he said.

I picked up the baseball from where Albert had dropped it into the grass. "Maybe we better not…"

"Hey, come on, it's my birthday!" Albert said.

Paul idly kicked at some tufts of dirt. "Oh, come on, don't be a sissy, Joe. It's Albert's birthday. Let's go. Just for a little while," he said.

It was nearly dark by the time we returned from the river. We ran into Albert's house hoping we weren't in trouble, but Aunt Leah said, "Come on boys—you're just in time." And I lucked out. My folks didn't get there until five minutes later. Mom didn't find out I disobeyed about the river. And yet, the feeling was still there. What had I forgotten?

The kids ate "Sloppy Joes" and potato chips and drank soda-pop. And as usual, the tables were groaning with my mom's special lasagna; with green salads; with yellow Jell-O; celery and pineapple salad; and broccoli casserole. The other aunts brought the sweets: cupcakes, pumpkin pie, and cream puffs.

The big moment came when it was time to blow out the candles. 16 of them were stuck into Albert's all-time favorite: yellow cake with marshmallow frosting flecked with toasted coconut and finely grated orange rind, and a wobbly "Happy Birthday Albert!" written in skinny blue frosting. As he took a big breath, some of the uncles yelled, "Come on Albert, get 'em all!" And he did.

That night the three of us horsed around in our makeshift sleep-out camp in Albert's room until nearly midnight. Finally we fell asleep.

In my dream, I heard the sirens and the crackling of the fire. The horrible red glow was all around me. Then Paul grabbed my arm, "Joe, wake up! Your house is on fire!"

What!

We ran down the street toward my house. I felt as if my legs were dragging through mud, as if I were running through chest deep water: This cannot be real, I thought.

Black smoke and orange flames leapt high above the trees. When we got there, it was already over. It was already done.

Where is my family? What happened to them?

∼

At the cemetery five coffins were lowered into the ground: one for my mother, one for my father, and one each for my three brothers. The sky was gray and drizzly as the final words were spoken by the priest. I looked up from the graves and saw Ava standing under a tree, on a shady bluff away from the crowd that had gathered to bid my family farewell. She wore a tan, hooded rain coat I had never seen before.

As the crowd filtered out, drifting back toward the waiting cars, I told Paul to go on ahead—I'd follow him in a few minutes. I walked up the hill to Ava. Tears trickled down her face. She took two steps toward me, her hands held out. "Joe, I'm so sorry," she said.

I was so angry.

"Sorry for what?" I asked. "The good luck you promised?"

Her hands dropped to her side. "For your family—for you—if I can help…"

"Help with what? More of your magic? More of the dreams you made me have again?"

Her face was completely still.

"Did you have the fire dream again?"

"What do you think?"

"I think you did. Why didn't you tell me?"

I took a step closer. "And what if I did, would it have mattered? I thought there was nothing you could do about a message in a dream."

She seemed to have shriveled, to have shrunken in size even as we stood there.

"I told you there was nothing I could do about my dreams, not yours," she said, "I told you to tell me if you had any dreams that disturbed you. This didn't have to happen."

"I don't believe you. I don't believe in anything you tell me. You're nothing but an old witch. I wish my mother would have never brought me to meet you. Your symbols and signs are bullshit. The one you gave me is burned along with everything else I loved. Don't do me any more favors, okay?"

Ava pulled her raincoat tightly across her chest.

"Don't you see, Joe? You have special gifts. Don't take the time we spent together lightly. You were about to have a breakthrough—if only we had more..." she shook her head. "Oh no, I didn't mean that," she reached toward me. "You can still..." She turned away from me then turned back. "Don't give up on your destiny, Joe."

I couldn't help it. I jumped back violently—away from her. "Destiny!" I screamed. "What makes you think anyone has a destiny? Was it my family's destiny to die like this? And what makes you think you know my destiny? You, with your long lost symbols and strange visions, you think you can tell me what my destiny is? My destiny is my business. My destiny is my life, and it doesn't have anything to do with you or your bullshit symbols and magic. I don't believe in destiny."

Ava turned from me—then looked back over her shoulder.

"That's your choice," she said.

"I'm finished with you," I told her. "I don't want anything to do with you or your strange magic. You're nothing but a witch. I never want to see you again. Do you hear me — never, ever again!"

She stood and looked at me, tears streaming down her cheeks.

"I understand Joe, I understand. Our work together — maybe it was too much. Maybe you weren't ready. But I can't change what has already begun. I will see you again, Joe. One day. It's our destiny." She walked away, down the hill, as the drizzle became a full rain.

~

Paul's family took me in and made a new family for me. My aunt and uncle took care of the details of the estate and the disposition of my father's medical practice. Though we lived in a small, blue-collar town, and were mostly working class people, there was enough money to assure I would have a good education and attend a proper university. I engrossed myself in the events of high school and college. There was even a bit of money from the estate to help me make my way into the world.

It was many years before I thought again about Ava.

WITH THE ANGELS

The child is getting restless now. He fidgets with his buttons. I watch him. And I sigh.

That's sad about his family, the child says. Will the little boy remember any of this when he arrives?

I don't know how to answer. How can I tell him that he may not remember anything about this story or this place? How can I explain that the only way to remember this place is with the heart?

Yes, of course he'll remember, I say. There will be reminders. He might hear a song. He might see a butterfly or a rainbow. He might have a dream. There will be reminders. There will be things that will help him remember where he came from.

The child picks up a long, slender leaf that has fallen from the willow tree. Then he looks up at me.

But will I remember you?

I look into the sky and take a deep breath. I can hardly speak.

One day, perhaps you'll be sitting under a tree like this and the wind will blow and the leaves will shimmer. Perhaps you'll look up into the sky and your breath will flutter. And perhaps in that brief tiny moment when all is still, if you listen with your heart, you'll remember.

ALBERT

Albert sat on a bench outside the Pavilion at North Shore Park. It was around two in the afternoon; we'd been there since mid-morning, as we'd been almost every Saturday that summer before my junior year of high-school.

I was inside the Pavilion playing a game of poker on a picnic table with three of my friends. Paul was inside too, near the snack bar with a group of girls, not too far from Albert. Paul was trying to act cool. He was trying to impress a girl he liked. I could tell. I knew Paul. I knew his moves. I knew the way he flexed his muscles when he tried to impress a girl. The movement was subtle. It was an unconscious thing — a little twitch. He couldn't help himself. The same way Albert couldn't help himself with the little twitches and spasms he had. He was born with them.

But Paul wasn't born with his twitch, his flex. He just did the unconscious movement when he tried to impress someone, especially a girl. He looked down at his biceps, which were protruding mightily since he'd been working out with weights the past couple of years. He didn't even realize he did it. But I realized it. And I watched him that day. I watched him, keeping my other eye on Albert.

Some of Paul's friends — or at least the boys who thought they were his friends — stood around Albert. They were too shy to talk to girls, so they hung out in a pack. Albert seemed to be fair game that day. A husky boy in a white tee-shirt and red swim trunks strolled up and taunted him. The boy moved his hands and jerked his head back and forth, mimicking Albert.

Oh yeah, I knew this guy in the red trunks. I'd seen him around town in the summer and on holiday breaks when he was home from boarding school somewhere in New England. His family owned some of the businesses that employed a lot of people in our area. He always seemed to think he could do whatever he wanted whenever he wanted to do it.

Albert tried to ignore the boy.

But Red Trunks kept it up. He was looking for trouble.

I saw the fight coming. It had happened many times before. First a little shove then a push, another push, another shove, and then the punches.

I'd stuck up for Albert so many times I'd lost track. But that day, I was tired, and I had a winning hand. I was hoping Paul would handle it; after all, he was only ten yards away from our cousin. But Paul was too busy being cool.

Another boy, a short boy wearing a New York Yankees baseball cap stepped out from the group and tried to figure out how to impress the girls. Shorty mocked Albert. He made spastic motions with his head and hands; he blinked his eyes rapidly to imitate Albert's involuntary eye movements. Albert, taller than Shorty, stood up. Shorty hesitated for only a moment and pushed Albert back onto the bench. Even though I couldn't see it, I knew the look on Albert's face: confused, still hoping it wouldn't go any further. Shorty pretended to poke Albert in the eye. Albert flailed out. Shorty jumped back.

Somebody shouted, "You're a freak!"

I don't know which spineless idiot said that, but it had gone too far.

What the hell was Paul doing? I knew he saw what was going on. He could have been there in three seconds to kick some ass. He knew none of those boys would mess with him.

Albert lunged for Shorty. Shorty curled into a crouch, and Albert flew right over him, landing face first in the sand.

The other boys laughed.

I slammed my poker hand down on the picnic table and broke into a run. I was pissed. I was going after somebody and I didn't care who it was. Red Trunks saw me coming and took two steps backwards. By that time, I was in his face. I grabbed the front of his tee-shirt and jerked him toward me.

"If I ever see you anywhere near my cousin again, I'll rip your head off!"

Red Trunks gave me a shove to the chest and broke my hold. "What's the matter with you man? I didn't do anything. We were just havin' some fun!"

I let my arms drop to my side, but my fists were clenched. "Having fun—my ass! He wasn't bothering anyone. Just leave him alone."

Red Trunks pulled at his tee-shirt, straightening it. "Alright! Alright!"

He turned and walked toward the group. He shook his head side to side. "What the hell's up with him?" The group scattered as I glared at them.

Paul was just behind me. I swung around to face him. "Are you sure you're cool enough, Paul? Are you too cool for Albert now too, or are you just going to pretend you don't even know him anymore?"

Paul threw out his arms in exasperation. "Look Joe, it's time Albert learns to take care of himself. We're not always going to be around."

"But you're around now."

It hurt me to be at odds with any of my close friends and especially a cousin, but I should have taken that stand with Paul a while ago. He had been distancing himself from Albert over the past year. I turned away from Paul and walked the few feet to where Albert was standing with a blank look on his face. "Hey, come on buddy, let's go get some fries."

I slung my arm around Albert's shoulder and looked back at Paul. "You coming with us?"

~

That day, because of Albert, I decided I would never allow anyone I loved to be treated poorly again. That day, I decided that I would do whatever it took to prevent this. That meant power. And that meant money. That's the way the world is. There are those who have power and there are those who are victims of it. I was going to have power, and I was going to have money.

The Light Place

The woman in the rose dress holds her hand palm facing down, a few inches above my head. She holds it there then glides it over the length of my outstretched body, over the blanket that covers me, all the way to my toes, then back again, slowly, meticulously, never touching me.

I gaze at her, a question in my eyes.

Creamy blue light streams in through the window. The pillow, the covers, and the canopy, the pastel shades of primrose and lilac mix with the light and fill the room with a glow.

"You're all right. You're right here, where I said you would be. Did you dream?" she asks.

She watches me.

"Was that a dream?" I ask. "I saw myself. I saw my family. They're looking for me."

She smiles and reaches over to guide me from the bed. Did she hear what I said?

"Come with me."

I stand. But I can't feel the floor beneath my feet. She holds my hand and leads me back to the room with the table and chair. The light fills this room, too. A gray and black long-haired cat lays curled on the sofa. I look for the picture of the cat hanging above the sofa, but it isn't there anymore. The cat on the sofa licks its paws and rubs its ears.

"Do you know what's happening yet?" she asks.

"I'm dreaming this whole thing, right?" I answer. "This is all a dream. You, this room, the little boy, the cave in the snow, it's all a dream, right? I'm going to wake up, it's going to be time for Christmas Eve, and this is going to be over."

"Oh yes. Soon it will be Christmas Eve. And everyone is waiting to see you," she says. Then she pauses. "But no, Joe, this is not a dream. This is more real than anything you have ever known. Do you understand?"

I don't know if I understand or not. Something about what she's saying is familiar to me. But what I have always known to be true before has a tenuous balance right now. The black and white world I lived in has shifted and taken on meanings I'd never imagined. Nothing is simple anymore.

There's a part of me that knows exactly what she's talking about. But I don't want to know it. And this woman — I want desperately to remember her. But it is just beyond my reach. Just beyond my awareness.

"No, I don't understand," I answer.

She takes a step toward me, and caresses my face. "There's something here for you to discover. The little boy has something for you. But you must be patient. This is your transition."

What does she mean by "transition?" If she means I'm dying, why doesn't she come out and say it? I've always hated that new-age babble. Anyway, I'm not going anywhere except back to Paul's house.

The woman stands on her tiptoes and moves her face toward mine.

"There's someone who wants to see you," she says.

She presses her lips against my cheek, and white light flashes before my eyes. The light explodes into tiny particles. Then everything is gone and I'm standing on a mountain top.

~

I'm standing on a snow-covered peak. Dim lights glow from the valley below. I think I had just been in a cottage down there. But I can't be sure. It's getting dark.

Off in the distance, I see something moving toward me, an animal or a small person making its way up the mountain. As it gets closer, the image is clearer. It looks like a man. As he approaches, the air gets colder. He's wearing brown and black fur boots and a brown fur coat with a hood that covers his head. Brown leather straps from the pack on his back crisscross his shoulders. His heavy dark-brown beard and straggly brown hair nearly obscure his eyes. He stops several feet in front of me and stands for a moment.

"They told me I would find you here," he says. He twists his shoulders and his backpack falls to the ground. He unties a pouch on the side of the bag, and pulls out a piece of fur the size of a loveseat throw. He hands it to me. "Wrap this around you," he says.

The temperature has dropped dramatically. I wrap as much of my body as possible, trying to cover my face and head.

"Follow me."

We walk in silence. He leads, I trundle close behind. I see a small wooden cabin. His pace quickens as we approach it. When he opens the door, snow falls from the roof onto our shoulders.

"In here," he says. He tells me to sit in a chair covered with animal fur. He sits next to me. He pulls his hood down around his neck. Ice crystals cling to his thick beard. He sits back in the chair and loosens his fur coat.

"Hello Joe, remember me?" he asks.

I rest my hands on my legs and look at him closely. Something feels painful about this. I look away and survey the room, buying time. The cabin walls are made of thick, round logs, held together with white mortar. The wooden floor creaks as I shuffle my feet and shift in the chair. I look back at him. "No, I don't remember you," I answer.

He rubs his hand over his beard to shake the water and ice away. Then he runs both hands over his long brown hair, starting at his forehead and squeezing the water out all the way to his shoulders, shaking the water off his hands.

"That's because when you knew me, I didn't look like this. The long hair and beard happened after I hit the streets." He pauses. "Do you know what's happening to you, Joe?" he asks.

I straighten up, and sit on the edge of my chair. "I'm not sure."

He lifts himself by the arms of his chair so that he, too, sits stiffly and at attention. Then he leans forward. "That's what I thought. I'm going to show you some things," he says. "I know you want answers. It was the same for me

when I first came here. It took a little while, but I figured
it out. And now I'm here to help you figure it out too."

He pauses and moistens his lips. "Then maybe I can get
off this mountain," he says.

What is this about?

He picks up a book that lay on the floor and takes it to
a bookcase full of old, leather-bound books. Next to it is a
black, cast iron, pot-belly stove, with a rusted flue.

"Is this place real?" I ask.

"Oh yeah, it's real alright. Right now you think it's a
dream, don't you? That's what I thought too. All I can tell
you now is that this is a transition place, a place for people
who haven't decided yet. You're here to decide. You're
lucky. Some don't get that chance."

He turns and looks out the window as if he's looking
for someone.

Did I hear that right?

"Decide…?" I lean forward to hear him better.

"Whether to live or die."

"What? Are you serious?"

He narrows his eyes. "Look, you're dying—okay? Isn't
that obvious?" he says. "I know what it's like though. You
feel like you're between two worlds. Part of you is here,
but another part of you is somewhere else. And you can't
make sense of it, can you?"

I nod my head. "Yes, yes! How do you know that?"

"Because I know how this works. I came here when it
was my time too. You have a choice to make. I'm here to

help you make it. I already made mine. And now this is my last task — to forgive you so I can move on."

I sit back in my chair and look up at the low ceiling, at the dark wooden beams that span the length of the room, and try to take in what he's telling me. "Forgive me for what?" I ask.

"My final illusion," he says. He sits down again, more relaxed this time, and eases into the fur chair's soft folds. "I was your first business partner Joe. Way back when you first started out. Remember?"

"Oh my god! Walt!" I open my mouth, but before any words come out, he stops me.

"No, don't say anything. It was a long time ago — another lifetime for me. We were just kids then trying to make it big. Remember now? New York. We both wanted to be big-time investment bankers. I got hurt in that car accident and had to take a few months off — remember now, Joe?

"The firm asked me to pick someone to handle my accounts while I was out. I trusted you to cover for me. When I came back, my clients wanted to stay with you. You had the gift of gab that I didn't have. You had the brains and the good looks too. You had everything going. And you stole my clients."

A jolt like an electric current shoots through me. Yes, I recognize him, and I remember. "But they wanted to work with me!" I say. "You could have had them back. You didn't try! You buckled! You didn't even put up a fight!"

"Oh, is that how you see it, Joe? Is everything just a fight? You lied. You made up stories about me to win over my clients." He takes a breath. "Just listen to me Joe. There's no need to put up a fight now. This is about me forgiving you. It's my illusion not yours. You don't have to rationalize it. It's just the way business was done at that firm in those days. It was the work we chose. But you didn't know what became of my life."

He rubs his hands over his long hair again. "You pressed ahead and forgot about me. But every life we touch intersects, Joe. Every action goes out and comes back.

"A year later you left for another firm—took all 'your' clients with you. You were on your way to the big time. But not me—no, I lost my job because of you. Soon after you left, I got let go. Lack of productivity, they said—didn't hit my numbers. I went home to my wife that day: thought she would comfort me, encourage me, and stand by me. But she wasn't all that crazy about me to begin with, I guess. She married me because she thought I could provide a fancy life for her. So at the first hint of things turning sour, she bolted."

I bury my head in my hands. Oh my god. Was I responsible for this man's anguish and misery? Who else had I harmed with my ambition and drive for success?

"She hooked-up with a hot-shot attorney and about a year later filed for divorce. She took our daughter and she was gone. I went into a downward spiral—a real bad one, Joe—lots of drinking and drugs. Finally, after rehab didn't work, I ended up in a homeless shelter. Bouncing around drowning my troubles in cheap booze or whatever I could find until my liver gave out. I got sick, who knows what finally killed me: Does it matter? I died alone on the street two days before my forty-first birthday."

I can't face this. My head droops and I close my eyes. Please, please, let this end.

He grabs my arm. "Look up Joe. Look at me! I got sick and died because I couldn't forgive the people who hurt me, and I carried that anger deep down inside. When I first came here, I thought everyone else was responsible for my miserable outcome. I see how I blamed others for my misfortune: my wife, my friends, our former boss...

"So I had to forgive them. But first I had to see the illusion of it all and forgive myself. And that's what I've learned here—about illusion and forgiveness. And I've forgiven myself and everyone else, everyone except you.

"You see, I thought you were the one who was responsible for what happened to me. But now I know. It wasn't you. It was me. So here I am on this mountain for the last of it, to forgive you so I can move on."

He stands and walks to one of the windows near the door. He looks outside. What the hell is he looking for? I want to get up and say something to him, but I stay in my chair. Then he turns around and faces me, leaning against an old wooden desk.

"I had dreams when I was young. I wanted to be a teacher and live a simple life. You know—a small town, part of a community. I loved working with kids. I could have been a great mentor. But something happened. I got seduced by money. So I put those dreams on a shelf for the pursuit of a high powered career. I guess I thought I couldn't do both."

He looks down and shakes his head and laughs. "I didn't follow my heart. I chased after something else instead—and for what? To impress my friends? To win the heart of a woman who would never be happy with the real me? Doesn't make much sense does it? And when it didn't work out I blamed everyone but myself. Do you know how many people I could have helped?"

He rubs at the corner of one eye, like a little boy trying not to cry. "Well I do. I met a bunch of those people — met them all in one night, Joe. I got to hear their stories. I got to find out how I could have made a difference. Yeah, I had some of that special brew too. Its powerful stuff isn't it?

"Now let's talk about you," he says. "You got the clients. The big-hitters started to notice you. Then you got the promotion. That put you in a new league. Wealth and affluence came next. You got your big houses and fancy cars and you started building your walls — the kind of walls that keep you safe and invulnerable. Or so you think. But in reality you built walls that keep out the ones that love you most: your wife, your kids, your family, your friends…"

He shakes his head. He laughs. "Oh Joe, the things we do."

The room is getting dark. Walt turns back toward the window. After a moment he glances at a lantern sitting on the desk. He snaps his fingers and a yellow flame appears inside the lantern. He smiles as if he's proud of himself and surprised by being able to light it this way.

"Maybe there's someone you need to forgive? Do you like lanterns Joe?"

What the hell is that supposed to mean?

I try to sort out everything he's telling me. I had forgotten about that time in my life and about this man in

the room with me. He was an insignificant memory—or so
I thought. Just another person I had stepped over in my
pursuit of success.

"You could say that I gave you your start," he says.
"You had the life I thought I wanted. But it wasn't true. I
see that now. Let's be honest about what we were doing in
those days. We were chasing the money—thought we
could buy a piece of the good life. The ego sure is a hungry
bastard, isn't it? Funny how some of us put our dreams on
a shelf, thinking we can pull them down one day after we've
'made it.' But while we're making it, things change, huh?
There's a price for making it, Joe. We both paid it—in
different ways."

His words cut into me like a scalpel, deep and clean.
I just sit and listen. What else can I do?

He shakes his head and walks back to the chair, picks
up his backpack and swings it over his shoulder. He walks
toward the door and stands there for a moment. Then he
turns around and looks at me. "You'll get a second chance
if you decide to take it," he says. "I traveled a long way to
tell you that you have a chance to change it all. You have a
choice. But I came here for me too, to make it all right—
because that's the way it works. Oh yeah, we really do reap
what we sow—all of it."

He reaches toward the door handle, but before he
opens it he looks back at me. "I'll be around Joe. You
may not see me but I'll be watching you. I'll be here until
you decide."

Walt opens the door. Snow blows into the room. I hold
up my hands to shield my eyes from the light. "Oh, I almost
forgot," he says. "That village down in the valley, where

the cottages are—there's going to be a party—maybe I'll see you there."

I jump from my chair and bolt toward him. "Wait!" I say. "We're not finished. You can't leave yet! What about my choice? How much time do I have to make it? And anyway, you're wrong. It wasn't all that way."

He opens the door and steps into the white space. "It was that way, and it's finished. I forgive you Joe. It's up to you now. Take a look," he says.

Then he's gone.

~

Is it the snow blowing into the room or am I in an entirely different place now? Whiteness encircles me. Then the image forms: I see myself in my mid-thirties sitting at my desk in my office. Is this what Walt meant when he said take a look? I can hear my thoughts. I can hear the words I speak and the words others speak to me. And I can see myself as if I'm watching a movie:

All I've got to do is close this last deal. If I can do this, I'll be the top dealmaker in the firm. And that means a hefty bonus and lots of stock options. If I can just close this last deal and get a few things signed before the end of the day, I can make it. I can hit my goal. I know I can do this. I just have to stay focused and get this one last deal done. This is what I've been working toward for the past five years. It's all come together for me now. If I can do this, nothing can stop me. I'll be able to buy that house and that new Mercedes convertible I've had my eye on.

These are my thoughts on this summer day as I sit in my office and work feverishly on the task before me. With a cold cup of coffee by my side (my fifth of the day) and papers scattered across my desk, I have one thing on my mind—closing this deal. Then it happens. My secretary pops in and tells me my mother-in-law is on the line. She says they think Jessica has gone into early labor, but not to worry, they're leaving for the hospital.

I tell Jesse's mother I'll meet them there as soon as I can. But I just can't seem to pull myself away. Come on, I tell myself, this is your new baby. What's more important, hitting your goals or being with Jessica for the birth of your child—okay, one more call to the attorney to button up that last item in the document and that's it—then I'm on my way.

But I'm still sitting at my desk. The attorney said he would call right back. I look at my watch. Holy shit! That was over an hour ago. The phone rings. It's Jesse's mother. I'm on my way, I tell her. Okay, I've got to get out of here. I frantically pack up my papers and stuff them in my briefcase. The phone rings again. It's the attorney. He got the call from the client. It looks like we're going to close the deal.

This is great news! There's just one minor snag. Our client will only do the deal if we agree to change some of the language and numbers in the prospectus that relate to their accounting practices. Although I know they follow the letter of the law, I also know they sometimes deviate from the spirit of the law. Their methods are complicated, and they use novel ways of characterizing income, assets, and liabilities.

Our attorney asks me if I will agree to the terms. If I don't agree, we won't get the deal done. What do you want me to do, the attorney asks. I tell him I'll call him right back. I think about it for a few minutes. My head is spinning. I really need to get to the hospital. I pick up the phone and call the attorney back and tell him I agree. The attorney asks if I can do one last thing. Sure, I can do that. It should only take me about twenty minutes. Sure I can get back to him within half an hour.

But I told Jesse's mother I was on my way. Oh hell, if this delivery is like the last one I've got plenty of time. Jesse was in labor for eight hours before she delivered John. And besides, her mother is with her. I'll get this last item knocked out and get over there.

I call the attorney back and give him the information he needs. I look at my watch. Oh no, how did this happen? I told Jesse's mother I would leave three hours ago. I wonder why she didn't call me again. Everything must be okay or she would have called. But what the hell's wrong with me? I've got to get out of here. I've got to get to the hospital — now! It's just a short drive from my office. I'll be there in no time.

I drive the three or four miles to the hospital. The traffic is light tonight. It takes me less than ten minutes. Alright, that's not so bad. I'm only a couple hours later than I said I would be. Jesse's used to me showing up late. She won't be too mad. Hell, I probably even have time to stop by the gift shop and buy her some flowers. That'll make her happy.

I buy the flowers and head up to the second floor. I ask the nurse where Jesse's room is and she tells me it's just down the hall — room 210. But when I walk into the room,

I see that Jesse is alone and crying. "Jesse, what's going on?" I ask.

She doesn't answer. She just waves her hand back and forth few times—waving me away. And she's crying into a ball of bunched up tissues. I set the flowers on the tray near her bed and sit on the bed next to her. She raises her hand to push me away. "Jesse, what's wrong? Is everything okay? Where's your mother? Are you alright?"

She doesn't speak. She covers her face with her hands. She's trembling and sobbing.

"Jesse! Tell me what's going on? Is the baby okay?"

But she can't talk. She's sobbing too much. I dash out of the room to the nurse's station. I talk to the first person I see: a young woman in blue scrubs.

"Can you tell me what's going on with my wife? She's in room 210, and she's sobbing. Is my baby alright?"

The woman looks at me, and pauses for only a split second. "Yes sir, she says. "Congratulations! You have a brand new baby boy. As far as I know, everything is just fine—the baby's adorable, and just as healthy as can be. I wasn't here for the delivery, I just came on duty a little while ago," she says. "He was delivered about an hour ago. I understand it was smooth as silk—that boy just popped right on out. Your wife's mother is in the nursery with the baby right now. They should be bringing him back soon. You can go to the nursery. It's just down the hall and to the left. Just follow the signs."

The nurse sets her clip board on the countertop. She tilts her head to one side and looks at me. "Hey mister, you just getting in from out of town or something?" she asks. "I don't know why your wife is crying so much. She's probably just happy, that's all. It's a pretty emotional time for a woman after a new baby comes. Just give her some lovin', she'll be fine."

I don't know where to go first. I want to see my new son. But something tells me I better get back to Jesse's room. Although now I know why she's crying so hard, and I really would rather go to see the baby and not have to deal with Jesse's emotions. But I head back to Jesse's room.

By the time I get there, Jesse's composed herself. Now she sits up in her bed with a cold blank stare. She folds her arms across her chest as I approach. The body language is quite clear. I sit in the chair next to the bed. And we're both silent for awhile.

"Is making money so important to you?" she asks. "Is it so important that you couldn't be here for your son's birth? My god Joe, what's become of you? My mother called you twice. Twice! You're less than ten minutes away. That was over three hours ago! What were you doing?"

I hang my head and try to disguise the fact that I'm flexing it to relieve the stiffness. I slide my eyes toward Jessica and see tears trickling down her cheeks. "I'm so sorry Jesse. I don't know what to say. I feel just as bad as you do. Do you think I didn't want to be here?"

Jessica turns away from me and looks out the window. She wipes her eyes and turns back toward me. "Are all your deals and accomplishments worth the price? Huh? Tell me now, because I need to know."

She is facing me. But her eyes are far away. I don't even know if she really sees me. Her eyes are red and puffy.

She sniffles a few times and blows her nose softly into the tissues. "None of that is important to me," she says. "Not if it drives a wedge between us Joe, and that's exactly what it's doing. Enough is enough. I've had it! I couldn't give a shit about that big house you've been talking about. Who are you doing this for anyway, Joe? How much do you need? What are you trying to prove?"

I don't have any words to comfort Jessica. And I fear that something in our relationship has been changed forever. I stand up and try to sit next to her on the bed. She raises her hand in protest, but I don't relent. I move onto the bed and put my arms around her. I kiss her softly on her cheek and her wet, salty tears run across my cheek. She hugs me back, but it's a tentative kind of hug. The kind that says irreparable damage has been done.

~

Then whiteness again. And a voice.

"I understand Joe. You thought money would give you power. Put that in your file of illusions. It doesn't work that way my friend. Money in your world may be everything, but in this world it's nothing. The only thing that matters here is love."

Walt, is that you? Walt?

Maybe Walt was right about me after all. But there was more. Another scene flashes before me: I wake up late, anticipating something. Something's in the air. I can feel it in the way the breeze rustles in the trees and the sultry summer heat simmers in my loins.

It's the Fourth of July. I'm going to a picnic at Uncle Lou's. We've had family picnics there on Independence Day for as long as I can remember. There'll be the aunts, the uncles, the little kids chasing each other with sparklers, and the long tables of chicken, and ribs, and coleslaw, and sausage and peppers, and pasta and peas, and greens and beans.

Is my white tee-shirt with the Sigma Chi emblem clean? I think I'll wear my khaki shorts and flip-flops. I grab the six-pack out of the fridge, (good, no one drank any of it!) zip out the front door to the driveway, open the door of my cool blue '66 Mustang, and toss the beer into the backseat.

I squeeze my car into one of the last spots at the field where the picnic is already at full roar. Paul is standing in his favorite spot: hovering over a makeshift grill of stacked cinder blocks and a metal grate, slapping on the barbecue sauce.

"Hey Joe, it's about time you got here," he says. "Late night last night? Who was she?"

I don't even answer that one.

I see Albert sitting by himself under a tree. I walk over.

"Hey, why are you sitting here all alone?" I ask.

Albert looks up quickly and then stares down at the gray blanket he's sitting on. "Oh, hey Joe. I don't know. I'm not feeling too good today," Albert says.

I squat next to him and put my hand on his shoulder. "Hey, come on now. It's the Fourth of July. You're supposed to be having a good time."

Albert looks up at me. His eyes are watery and puffy and I know he's been crying.

"Hey, what are the tears for?"

"I don't know Joe. I've just been so sad lately. I feel like I don't fit in anywhere in this world." Albert rubs his fingers over his eyes. "What's wrong with me Joe? I just want to be normal."

I put my hands on Albert's knees and then I take his hands and pull him up. "Come on now," I say. "I'm not going to let you sit here by yourself all day today. Let's go get up a game of bocce. Come on, you and I will be on the same team. We'll kick some butt just like always."

Albert smiles and stands and follows me and we get up a game. I'm worried about him. But I don't know what to do.

From time to time, as the day wears on I almost forget that feeling of the morning. But it keeps coming back, something sweet and sensual, like melted chocolate, warm and moist in my mouth.

As a kid, I would stick around until dark and go with my family to watch fireworks, but today by early evening, I'm ready to leave. At home I consider taking a shower and going to bed, but instead I decide to go out.

About ten o'clock I head out to "The Sunken Treasure." "The Treasure," as it's known by the locals, is an old dance hall converted a while ago to a rock-and-roll club on the strip at Harbor Cove. The "Strip" is a little over a mile long. It's just a short hike up a shady hillside from the beach down by the lake.

In its heyday, the old-timers say—in the mid-1940s— the Strip would be lined with Fords, Oldsmobiles and Packards. The old-timers still talk about the summer Tommy Dorsey, Cab Calloway, and the young Frank

Sinatra came through: Cars were backed up for miles on both sides and you couldn't get near the place.

It must have been something back then, I think, as I park my car and look down the Strip. It's a bit run down now. The once famous Flying Jets, the Dodge'ems, and the Penny Arcade have been replaced by rickety hot dog stands, dingy donut shops, and seedy bingo parlors. Signs that mark the most prominent establishments, once lit up with dazzling displays, now have burned out lights and missing bulbs. And yet, this night, the Strip has a charm and character that is classic. This night, the orange and green neon signs, the pink and yellow blinking lights, the red, white, and blue faded flags, are magical.

Tonight, The Treasure is packed with teenage kids, young adults, and lots of out-of-towners. The under-18 crowd loiters around the entrance, and occasionally a few lucky ones make it past the bouncers checking ID's. There seem to be a lot of kids fresh out of college here tonight, like me.

The outdoor patio is crowded. Tonight's local band is making their usual mess of the Rolling Stones' "Satisfaction." You'd think they could try a new song to slaughter, I think. Inside, it's bustling and noisy, and kids are dancing. I hang out with some of my old high school pals for awhile and some guys who made it back from Viet Nam. Luckily, my lottery number was 256. I don't think I'll be going. A few of my friends didn't make it back.

Some of the kids are dressed in the usual Ivy League attire. Others are wearing bell bottom pants, and hip-huggers with embroidered shirts and wide belts, or leather fringe jackets or vests. Some girls wear soft muslin blouses, embroidered with flowers, and love beads or headbands. The air smells like stale beer and cigarette smoke.

It's been a long day. Too many beers already in the hot sun and I've got to get up early. No more drinking and partying tonight. What am I doing here anyway? I haven't had a drink since around seven o'clock, and I'm starting to fade. It's hot, there's no air conditioning in this place. It's more than hot, it's stifling. So I walk out onto the patio to get some fresh air. The patio's about the quarter size of a basketball court. Most of it is filled with people. I can hear the muffled sound of go carts and the faint screams of kids on the new roller coaster ride down the Strip.

I push through to the railing and stand with my back to the crowd looking out at the lake. I take one last drag from my cigarette and flick the ashes into the stones and dirt in the corner where the silhouettes of bushes are. The sky is dark.

Something tells me to turn: the same something that's been following me around all day; the same something I can't quite seem to grab onto; the same something that brought me here tonight. But I fight the urge and continue to look into the black sky.

The sensation is overwhelming, though. So I give in.

I turn around. And there she is: standing with a few other girls.

I've never seen her here before, but there she is: tall and thin, light blue bell bottoms and white sleeveless blouse, wide white belt, shoulder-length golden-blonde hair. She doesn't look like a local. She glances at me and our eyes meet, but I look away. What's this — I'm a little shy tonight? Maybe I should get that drink after all — get my courage up.

The blonde walks away from her group toward a table where a dark-haired girl sits. They lean toward each other over the table, giggle, and then glance at me. When they see I'm looking, they look away. A little more giggling, they glance my way again, then avert their gazes. Classic mating ritual. I think I need that drink.

Brown Hair motions for me to come over.

Who me? You want me?

Yes you. She nods, and makes a subtle motion with her hand. The blonde giggles. She gestures for her friend to stop. But Brown Hair keeps waving me on.

Okay… Okay… I take a few steps toward the table. Brown Hair stands up. She whispers something to the other girl. She looks at me and flashes a sly little smile, and walks inside.

Now what am I supposed to do? Are they playing a game with me? Is the blonde going to get up and go inside too? Then what? Do I follow them in? I can't turn back now. I truly wish I had gotten that drink.

I keep walking. The blonde turns toward me. Our eyes meet. Look at those eyes! She smiles. My heart flutters.

A few more steps. Come on, get hold of yourself, it's just a girl. But this isn't just any girl, and this isn't just any day. This is the Fourth of July, and I'm close enough to see the color of her eyes, and I swear those blue eyes are sparkling. Oh yeah, they're sparkling. Like a hundred firecrackers crackling, a thousand sparklers sizzling, a million roman candles exploding: diamonds in the midnight sky.

"Hi, I'm Joe," I say.

She dips her head and glances at me from underneath her silky hair. She opens her mouth and rose blossoms bloom. I swear I can see them. I'm intoxicated. I'm dizzy.

"I'm Jessica," she says.

I don't even know if I can talk. I think my mouth is frozen. Come on, there's got to be some words in there. Say something.

"Nice night tonight," I say. I look up into the black sky.

Oh come on, you can do better than that. You've been with plenty of girls. You're a veritable Casanova. Certainly, you can strike up a conversation with this girl.

She turns and looks back to see if her group is still there. But they've all scattered. Uh-oh she's nervous. She straightens up a bit and says, "Would you like to sit down?"

I move toward the seat next to her, trying to look cool. I'm not sure how close to sit. So I pull the seat a couple of feet away from the table—far enough to give her lots of space. "I hope I'm not bothering you," I say. "I thought I saw your friend motioning for me to come over. Where did she go?"

Jessica fiddles with the nearly empty glass in front of her. The candle on the table flutters and makes the blonde of her hair glisten. "Oh, she went inside," Jessica says. "She's had a bit too much to drink. She likes to play around like that, especially when she's drinking." She shakes her head to flip her hair out of her eyes. "It's embarrassing. I hope you don't mind. I think she thinks you're cute."

I lean a little closer to her. Your friend thinks I'm cute. What about you, I want to say. But I don't say it. I don't have the courage. This girl's got me flustered. But I've got to assert myself or I'll miss my chance.

"Well Jessica, I think you're cute," I say.

Jessica bats her eyes a few times, and turns her head away.

Holy shit! Where did that come from? Did I say that?

She looks back at me and I see those blue eyes again. Her cheeks are flushed and pink. She leans in a little closer and relaxes her shoulders. Now I notice the texture and shape of her lips, smooth and just slightly plump.

I scoot my chair a little closer.

"Well I think you're cute too," she says.

I touch one of her fingers. Gently. "Do you have a boy friend?"

Now where did that come from? What's gotten into me? This girl has gotten into me—that's what.

She frowns, just a little frown, and drops her head, just a little bit. "No, my boyfriend and I broke up a while ago."

"That's too bad," I say. "I know how that can be."

I make a decision, at this moment, to ask her out on a date. "Would you like to do something together sometime?"

"Oh, I would like that," Jessica says.

I nudge her playfully on the arm. "What kind of things do you like to do? Do you like to play miniature golf?"

"Oh, that would be a lot of fun!' It'll be okay if I don't get the ball in the hole very often, won't it?" She looks helpless and demure.

"Oh don't worry about that, "I say. "I'll give you some lessons."

I must be in heaven. This girl is really something.

~

"That was the luckiest day of your life Joe."

Walt?

Why did he show me that?

The light disappears and I'm back in the dark again

THE SNOW CAVE

The darkness of the snow cave closed in on me. Yet I remembered the place of light. I remembered its beauty and peace. The warmth, the cottage, the crystal snow, the boy, the woman in the rose colored dress, and most of all the light. I wanted to go back, but I didn't know how.

In the billowy fog of my mind, it seemed I was between two worlds just like Walt said. Part of me was here but part of me was somewhere else. Up to this point I had fought for life. I had been unwilling to let go. But now as my strength drained away I was losing my will to live.

It's over I thought. I can't fight anymore. As my hands slid to the frozen ground, I felt something in my jacket pocket. I fumbled at the zipper with my numb, swollen fingers. I reached in and pulled out a hard, round cylinder. A flashlight? Paul must have used this jacket recently on one of his snow plowing jobs, I thought, and left it in the pocket.

I pushed on the knob. Dim yellow light oozed out onto the walls of the cave. The faintness of the light, I thought, meant the batteries would soon be dead: just like me. But for the first time since I had fallen, I had a chance to see the place where I'd been trapped. I shined the light along the icy ceiling and the walls of the cave. I turned the light toward my face and watched my breath rise like a fog.

I pulled my jacket sleeve back and shined the light on my wrist. Six! Was it six in the morning or six at night? Could it be that I had only been trapped in the snow for three hours. Or was it the next day?

It didn't matter. I had light. I unzipped the other jacket pocket and reached in. I pulled out a lump of something and a piece of paper. I held them in the light. What's this? — a Snickers bar and a twenty-dollar bill.

Oh great, I thought, money — just what I need — a lot of good that's going to do me now. I rested the flashlight on my stomach and tried to open the Snickers wrapper, and as I did, the flashlight dimmed and the candy bar fell out of my hand.

In a fit of anger and exasperation, I hit the flashlight on the ground. The light flickered on and off. And each time the light flickered, my will to live flickered with it. When the light went out completely, I threw the flashlight. I heard it bounce, then nothing more.

I reached around on the frozen ground and tried to find the candy bar. I found it, but my fingers were too numb to open the wrapper. Damn, damn, that I had been so drunk out there in the storm that I threw my gloves away! So I bit through the wrapper into the half-frozen candy. A piece of the wrapper got caught in my throat and made me cough. Finally, exhausted, I drifted off to sleep.

~

"Well, this is quite a mess you've gotten us into, Joe. But don't worry, I'm here now."

What the hell is that? I struggle in the dark to see where the voice is coming from.

"Who's in here?" Warm air flows over me, the caress of exhaled breath flitters across my face. I sense the presence of something nearby. "Walt? Have you come to take me back?"

Ice particles fall on my face.

"I wish it was that easy Joe. But this isn't Disneyland. You're not in Fantasy Land anymore."

"Who are you? Show yourself!" Again, the warm breath. The smell of stale whiskey and cigarettes.

"This is real now, Joe. How long do you think you can hold out in here? Look at you. You're a mess. One too many shots—huh, Joe? You won't last another half-hour without me."

I wave my hand from side to side, but feel nothing. Why is this thing taunting me? Am I hallucinating again? "What do you want with me? Can't you see I'm hurt and trapped? Who are you? Are you a friend of the boy? Do you know the woman in the cottage? What about Walt?"

I thought I was out of this cold, dark place. Didn't the child lead me out? What happened to the warm bed? It can't be that I'm back in this goddamn cave again. I try to feel the surface around me. Sharp cold rock. Maybe whoever this is can lead me out. Maybe I can cut a deal with this thing.

"Okay, okay. I've made up my mind. I've made my choice—I want to go back to that place of light—I have friends there."

"Hah! You want to go back to the place of light, huh?—and see your friends? Well isn't that nice. Sorry buddy, they can't help you now."

Wild laughter echoes in the cave. I cover my ears with my hands.

What does he mean I can't go back? I thought Walt said I had a choice? Was there an expiration on the choice?

"You think you can just slide out of here and get into heaven. Oh no. No one gets into heaven for free. You've got to pay a price for heaven. Everything has its price, Joe. Everything is a deal. You know all about deals. Don't you, Joe?"

Heaven? Do they really call it heaven? Does that mean I'm in hell? I sink low to the ground, crouching, trying to evade the thing. Its voice seems to have grown louder—so loud that it shakes the walls and floor.

"What do you want?" I moan. "I'll give you anything?" I dangle the money in the air. "Take it! I'll give you whatever you want—whatever I have. Just get me out of here!"

Again, the wild laughter. I cover my ears and head. "Listen to him! He thinks he can buy his way out."

I push my hands against the frozen ground and lift my head to rest it against the wall. "Why do you taunt me? Who are you? Show yourself—goddamn it!"

It's quiet for a while. All I can hear is the thing breathing. In and out.

Then a dim light comes on in the cave—a single round light bulb dangles from a thin black cord. It hangs from the ceiling above my legs and casts a gloomy yellow glow on a huge thing sitting across from me.

The thing seems to have a head and body made of dark gray fog or mist, but at the same time it looks like a shadow. It fills the entire cave. It wears a dark overcoat and black hat that brushes against the cave's ceiling. A cigarette juts out from the place where its mouth should be.

"Who are you?" I cry. "What are you? All I can see is shadow."

"Oh, you should know me well by now, Joe. I've been with you a long time."

I rub my eyes. This can't possibly be happening.

"What's the matter? Still don't recognize me Joe? I'm the one who brought you your success, the one who drove you day after day, the one who taught you how to win, the one who helped you get all the things you wanted in your life. Without me, you'd be nothing. Oh, Joe," the thing says, sighing.

"The things I've done for you. You know, it's not easy being me, Joe—the unappreciated one. How would you like it? You really should be more gracious. You're the one who got us into this mess, and now you want me to get us out. That's the way it's always been—I don't know Joe, looks like the only way out is for you to die."

The shadow laughs its horrible laugh again. It takes another deep breath then exhales. The cave is silent. I dare not move or speak. I don't want to make it angry.

"What do you mean by that?" I whimper.

The shadow is calm now. "Don't worry Joe. I'm not going to let you die. Not without a fight. It's a good thing you're a fighter, Joe. You see, if you die, you go on. But not me. I'm not so lucky. I can't go on with you. I need you to stay alive until someone rescues us. I need you to keep feeding me, Joe.

"Right now I need you to fight for your life. Because your death is the end of me and I'm not going to let that happen."

With that the shadow sucks us up and out of the cave.

~

We float in the air above the street where I had lived as a child.

We hover for a while above my childhood home, then glide over the trees and rooftops half a block away to Albert's house. We hover outside Albert's bedroom window for a moment then float through the wall into Albert's room. This is the night of Albert's birthday party. I look at the shadow for some clue as to what's in store for me, but it doesn't look back. It just floats in the air, cigarette hanging from its gaseous mouth, arms folded across its chest.

"What are you going to show me, Shadow?"

It doesn't speak.

We're floating around in this room and no one can see us. But I see myself—I'm a teenager sleeping on the floor next to Paul and Albert—they're teenagers too. I gaze in disbelief and turn toward the shadow, when, without warning, it spins around and lifts us up through the ceiling of the house. There, in the darkness, I see the iridescent glow of a reddening sky.

Below us, the three boys race toward the reddish glow. A metallic clattering of sirens and bells fills the night air.

A fire truck screeches to a halt on the street in front of my house. Three firemen jump out. They pull a long gray hose off the truck and carry it to the house. They aim the hose and spray water at the flames roaring from the upstairs windows.

I'm watching a scene from my childhood. A memory I thought I had buried long ago.

"Oh no! Not this! Why are you showing me this?"

The shadow doesn't speak. We drift in the street in front of my house. And I begin to remember something — something I had forgotten I even knew. The lantern! Oh my god! The lantern! "It wasn't my fault. I didn't do it on purpose. I didn't!"

Small, glowing red circles, the size of quarters, appear in the place of the shadow's eyes. A darker, gray circle appears at its mouth. The faintest outline of a face begins to form.

"This is your guilt. Remember Joe? You were in the basement that afternoon. How many times did your father tell you not to play with that lantern? But you didn't listen. You loved to light that lantern, didn't you?"

"Yes, yes!"

"You forgot to turn the knob to extinguish the flame. You left the lantern on the table next to your father's workbench and ran out to go to Albert's party didn't you?"

"Yes, yes, I remember now!"

A dawning sense of horror rises in my chest.

"The dog knocked the lantern to the ground late that night." The entity says. "The glass burst, the kerosene splashed onto the wooden workbench. That's where the fire started. Your mother and father and your brothers were all asleep. Smoke and fire drifted up from the basement and filled the upstairs of the house."

"No. No more! I don't want to know. I don't want to see anymore. Please. No more. I beg you. Please." I can't turn away. I see my mother and father, and my brothers sleeping. I see the black smoke. It fills their bedrooms and billows out the windows. I see the flames lick toward the upper floor. I drop to my knees. I hold my head in my hands. I stand up. I run toward the house.

"Save them!" I yell to the firemen. "Please save them!" But just before I reach the firemen, I'm repelled by a force. I push hard against it. But I'm repelled again.

"Relax Joe, they can't see you—or hear you. We're not here to change what happened, Joe. They're dead."

No! No! No!

The firemen pull my family out of the house before the flames reach them. They place the bodies on the front lawn and pull gray covers over their heads. The bodies lie on the ground with gray covers over them and then I see my yellow blanket covering something else on the ground and I realize that something else is my dog Paddy.

I fall to my knees.

It was the lantern! Oh my god! I forgot about the lantern! Did I cause the fire?

The shadow fades away; the red eyes and gray mouth fade away. Its face becomes the face of a man.

I'm looking at myself.

"Guilt Joe, it's been with you a long time. You've carried the guilt of that day all of your life. Your earliest memories shaped your life Joe. Even when we think we can't remember, the memories stay with us and form our beliefs."

"I didn't do it! I didn't do it! It wasn't my fault!" I cry. "I should have been in the house with them! Why wasn't I there? Why did I have to go on living? I should have died with them!"

"You owe me one—because I made sure you weren't in the house that night, Joe. Don't you remember how you told your mother you thought Albert wanted a spend-the-night party for his birthday? Who do you think gave you that idea? It was me—I planned the sleep over at Albert's—I saved you—see how you owe me?"

"You son of a bitch!" I lunge at the shadow and swing my fist at his head. My fist flies through the mist; my body spins around. I swing again, aiming at what would be his chest. "You son of a bitch, I know who you are now—I don't owe you anything! All you've ever done is cause me pain! You're never satisfied are you? You want more and more and more. The more you have the more you want!"

The shadow is angry. His breath comes in spurts. "You didn't pay attention to me Joe. Hell, most of the time you didn't even know I was there. You ignored me. You buried me. All I wanted was for you to notice me. But it had to come to this—so unnecessary—so unnecessary. I'll tell you what. I'll make you a deal, Joe. I'll get you out of that hole in the snow," he says. "But if I get you out, you have to promise to keep feeding me—promise me you will. Do we have a deal?"

I swing my fist at his mouth this time. "Get away from me you son of a bitch. If I get out of that cave alive, the only thing I promise is to never listen to you again. I'll change my ways. You'll see. I'm the master of my life, not you. You'll never influence me again. I'll do whatever it takes to silence you. Do you hear me, you bastard?"

I swing again and the overcoat wraps around my arm. Then the thing disappears as my head slams against the hard, frozen wall of the cave. I cup my hands over my face and cry.

I look for the light. I look for the Shadow. But nothing is there: just me, and the cold dark night.

THE LIGHT PLACE

I hear Walt's voice and the white surrounds me again.

"Maybe you were right, Joe. Maybe it wasn't all that way. But you always had to have an angle didn't you? Always had to get what you wanted. But it's never enough is it? Not when your shadow is in charge. You know, Jessica was the best thing that ever happened to you."

Another scene flashes before me: The sultry end-of-summer days fly by until the first early signs of autumn signal winter's inevitable return. It's a warm and breezy late August day. It seems longer than just six weeks since Jessica and I met. We walk the narrow path of a steep embankment that leads to a beach behind the North Shore Boat Club. We make our way through tall grass and leafy trees. I hold Jessica's hand and guide her over small rocks and knobby roots. I show her where to place her feet and how to grab each branch so she won't fall.

This is my path, my territory, my place. I know it by heart. I know every twist and turn. Jessica is impressed — I think — but she doesn't let on. Not yet anyway; she's still watching me, watching to see if I'm real. Jessica isn't the first girl I've taken to this spot, but I don't mention that today.

The lake is rough. Whitecaps slap at the brown rocks of the uneven break wall. Cool water splashes in our face. Jessica laughs and grabs my arm. We walk hand in hand, stepping over cracks and crevices of the jagged blockade. Jessica says she's afraid of rats. I laugh, and tell her not to worry: They're not very big, I say, and even so, I'll protect you.

She smiles. We stop on a concrete embarkment that juts about twenty yards into the water. We walk to the middle. I lead. She follows. Still hand in hand. We get to the end of the embarkment and look out at the water. The sun is still high in the sky, but is beginning its descent into the horizon. The sunset on the water will be magnificent tonight if the wispy indigo clouds cooperate.

I point to a large cargo ship, barely visible, far out on the rim. It's probably carrying coal to Canada, I tell her. I snuggle up close behind Jessica and wrap my arms around her waist. She drops her hands onto mine. I kiss the back of her neck. She purrs as she relaxes her head and lets it fall back onto my shoulder. A warm heat rises from deep inside me. She turns. We embrace. The warmth spreads like fire. We kiss. The fire burns all the way to my heart.

~

It's dusk. The sun is down. We're the only ones on the beach. Dim strands of watermelon colored light cling to the last remnants of day on the horizon. We sit on a worn cotton blanket on lumpy sand close to the surf, gentle now that the wind has died down. Jessica says she's getting chilly. She snuggles close to me and we fall back onto the blanket into each other's arms. We kiss again: this time, a deep, sensual, passionate kiss.

She pulls away and looks into my eyes.

"I didn't want to fall in love with you," she says.

I pull her close, kiss her mouth and run my hand ever so slightly over her breasts, across her stomach and down the outside of her thigh, to her knee, and then up to the button on her shorts. She grabs my hand. "No," she says, "Someone might see us."

I take a breath.

"Don't worry, its dark now—there's no one around." I fumble around for that button again.

Jessica grabs my hand, rolls on top of me and bites my neck. She sits up gently on my stomach, supporting herself with her knees, resting her hands on my shoulders.

"We had an agreement," she says. "Just friends, remember? I'm way beyond that now, Joe, but I leave in a few weeks. I start my new job the middle of September. What about you? What are you going to do? If you take that job in New York, what's going to happen to us?"

I don't know what to say. I don't want to say anything. Can't we just have this time together? Why do girls have to have some kind of commitment? I reach up and slide my fingers through her silky, fragrant hair. I pull her face close to mine, and kiss her again. "Can't we talk about that later," I say.

She pulls away, lifts herself up on her knees again, and playfully pummels me on my shoulders with her fists. "I'm falling in love with you, Joe," she says. "I didn't want this to happen. The last thing I wanted was to fall in love on my summer vacation with a guy I barely know."

I tickle her lightly under her arms. She giggles.

"Oh come on—we've been going out for almost two months, we know each other pretty well by now," I say.

"You're just a drifter at heart aren't you?" she says, "You've got three offers on the table and you haven't made up your mind yet. You don't know what you want to do."

I sit up. "What do you mean? I know exactly what I want to do. I'm going to make a lot of money and be a huge success. I see it already. Hey, come on, we can stay in touch and visit each other on weekends once in a while until we get settled."

We lay side by side now. I rest my chin on my hand and look at her. Jessica tucks her hair behind her ear. "Oh right. A long distance relationship. How long do you think that'll last?"

I run my hand over her shoulder, down the curve of her hip, and let it slide around to the small of her back. "Hey, we're young. We've got lots of options. You could come with me. With your pedigree, you could get a job with any P.R. firm in the country."

"Yeah right," she says, "I'm going to follow some guy I just met all around the country until he figures out what to do with his life. My folks would love that."

Jessica and I roll onto our backs and look at the sky. The stars reveal themselves one by one as the black of night sets in. The Big Dipper is barely visible. Jessica touches my hand and rubs the tops of my fingers. We lay quietly for a long time looking into the sky and listening to the waves and the crickets. Then Jessica turns to me and speaks softly.

"The stars are so beautiful tonight. Aren't they Joe?"

"Yes, they are," I say.

Jessica softly squeezes my hand. Then she murmurs, "Have you ever heard the Eskimo proverb about the stars?"

"What's that?"

"It says: *Perhaps they're not stars, but rather openings in heaven, where the love of our lost ones pours through, and shines down upon us to let us know they're happy.*"

I drift away for a moment. What a beautiful thought. What a beautiful girl. I'm inside the cup of The Big Dipper, and I think about my family. I wonder where they are. I hadn't thought about them all day. That hasn't happened in a long time. I must really like this girl. I might as well admit it. I knew it the first time I looked in her eyes. "Hey, how do you know so much about Eskimo proverbs," I ask.

"I took a course my last semester in college on native American cultures. It was really cool."

I like this girl. I really do. I roll onto my side and rest my hand on her hip. I run my fingers under her shirt to her bare tummy. I kiss her softly and hold her close and whisper in her ear. "I love you, Jessica."

I breathe in the scent of her hair and skin and I swear rose petals are falling out of the stars. "I don't say those words too often, and I know we just met, but I want to be with you."

Jessica pulls me close. "I love you too Joe. And I want to be with you."

I hear the gentle swishing of the waves on the shore. We wrap the blanket around us. I fumble around for that button again. And this time, she doesn't stop me.

ALBERT

Albert was in trouble. Paul called to tell me. Several years after college, after I had left my hometown and set out to make my way in the world I received the call. Albert had gotten mixed up with a group of dead-beat guys, Paul said. That meant Albert had gotten involved with guys who were using drugs and getting high. Nothing too heavy. A little grass and stuff. Just passing time, he said, but still, they were a bunch of losers.

I was busy with my own life. I had just been promoted to a new position in the firm and I was traveling a lot. Jessica and I were married and our first child was on the way. There was no time to do anything for or about Albert. I told Paul there wasn't much I could do from where I was and I asked him to do what he could, but I knew Paul had distanced himself from Albert years ago. The days of our youth were gone forever. There's only so much one can do for another person. At some point along the way we each have to follow our own paths. And Albert's path led him to a strange place. A place his family couldn't understand. So they didn't get involved.

On the few occasions when I did get back to my hometown I tried to talk to Albert. But time and distance and growing up have a way of changing our trajectories. Albert had already built his walls around his new world—

his new friends. At least he had a group to hang with. Even if they were a bad influence.

And although I pretended he was okay, that he had found a home with the misfits and dropouts, I knew deep down he was in trouble. But I didn't know what to do. I didn't know how to help him. So I didn't do anything.

1995

Jessica walked in from the rain carrying a stack of mail. She told me earlier that morning she hadn't been down to the street to get the mail in three days—more than likely the result of her planning and coordinating the small group of friends who got together at our house to celebrate my forty-seventh birthday the night before. She placed the mail on the kitchen counter. She grabbed the edge of the counter with one hand and raised the other to her forehead. She pressed hard, and rubbed.

I stood in the corner—a little groggy from too much wine at the celebration last night. She didn't notice me.

"What's the matter baby, another headache?"

She jumped. Turning towards me she said, "Oh my god—you scared me! I didn't see you!" She sighed. "Oh, I'm okay—probably just the weather—you know, these rainy days."

I walked to her and rubbed her shoulders. "Poor baby—rainy days or too much wine? Anyway, you've been getting them pretty often lately. Maybe you should see a doctor."

She fumbled through the mail. "Oh, I'm sure it's nothing. I'm going to my GYN next month. I'll ask her about it then. Don't worry, I'm fine. Gee—seems like we've been getting a lot of credit card offers lately—doesn't it?" She scattered the stack of mail on the stone countertop, picking up random pieces, separating them into messy stacks.

I rolled up the sleeves of my gray sweatshirt—my typical Saturday morning attire—sweatshirt, shorts, and running shoes. "Yeah, I guess they think we have some money," she said.

I smiled. "We do."

She laughed.

"Hey, what's this?" she asked. "I can't make out the writing very well, but it looks like it's addressed to you— looks like it's from Switzerland. Who do you know in Switzerland?"

She pulled a small thin ivory-colored envelope from the bottom of the stack of letters and magazines and advertisements. The letter was marked "PERSONAL."

"I don't know." I shrugged. "I wasn't expecting anything."

Jessica held up the envelope and offered it to me. I took the envelope and held it in my hand for a while and looked at it. My name was etched in handwriting that seemed vaguely familiar. I studied it for a few seconds trying to recall where I'd seen the shape and style of the fonts. I didn't know if I should open it right here or take it into my study and read it in private.

"Well, aren't you going to open it?" Jessica asked.

I pulled the letter to my chest, playfully, trying to have some fun with Jessica—to take her attention away from the throb in her forehead. "But it says 'personal.'" I narrowed my eyes at her.

I pretended to walk away from the counter to see how Jessica would respond. But I was only half teasing. I really

didn't want to open the letter in front of her—it might be
something I didn't want her to see. But I didn't want her to
think I was trying to hide something from her, and besides,
it was probably just a new-fangled type of direct mail
solicitation from an aggressive stock jockey in New York.

"Oh honey, you've got to be kidding me—open it,"
she said.

I worked my finger underneath one of the corners of
the flap and tore it open. I took out the folded, heavy-
stock, ivory-colored paper. Inside was a handwritten note,
barely legible. I stood at the counter and read without
looking up at Jessica. What the hell is this? After the
second sentence I realized who the note was from. How
the hell did she find me?

Dear Joe,

*I hope this note finds you well. It's been a long time
since we saw each other. That wasn't a pleasant time for
either of us. So much has happened since then I don't know
where to begin. I've already said I'm sorry so it seems there
are no more words to say about that.*

*I'm getting old now and I'll be leaving this world soon.
I'm sure you remember the symbol I gave you—there are
three if you recall. I had a dream last night and now I know
for certain that you are the one I'm to give them to. There are
others who know now. Maybe you'll find them. I remember
what you said that day so I'll understand if you tear up this
note and throw it away and forget about me forever.*

*I buried a package near the oak tree next to the rose
trellis where the robin used to make its nest. Remember? I*

know you do. Look for a stone cross. You are the only one who knows where it is.

Follow the instructions Joe. Fulfill your destiny. I hope you will.

Love, Ava

I dropped the note on the counter and stared at it. I'd been transported to another time. I looked at the note but I could've just as easily been looking into the center of the Milky Way.

Jessica had been watching me, quietly. "Who's it from Joe?"

Memories surged through me. A rush of heat pressed against my chest and into my head, an anvil dropped from Mount Everest and landed in the center of my gut. I didn't answer Jessica's question.

"What is it Joe?" She placed her hand on my arm.

I couldn't think. I couldn't talk. I couldn't move.

"Joe, what's wrong? Are you alright?"

I didn't know what to say. I didn't know what to do. I thought I had buried the memory of this woman and that strange time in my life somewhere in a cavern under a coral reef off the coast of Australia.

How did she find me? How does she know where I live?

I grabbed the edge of one of the high-backed swivel chairs near the counter and fell into it.

"Joe, what is it?" Jessica put her hand on my shoulder and reached for the note. "Are you okay?"

I covered the note with my hand then looked up at her.

"What's the matter?" Jessica asked. "Who's it from? What does it say?"

I put my hand on top of hers. "Oh, Jesse, I think we have to talk."

I took Jessica's hand and lead her into the family room. I guided her to the couch and sat down beside her, turning so I looked straight into her eyes. I know she didn't know what to think. It seemed as if we had just walked three miles—at least I've had time to think about what to say; how to explain the letter; how to frame everything so that she'd understand what this note meant without thinking she's married to some kind of nut job out of a science fiction movie.

What am I going to say? Is it fair to Jesse to bring her into this? And do I even want her to know? But I don't want to hide things from her—where do I begin? I took a deep breath. I looked in her eyes. I waited for the words to come.

Let me see. When I was young I used to have weird dreams and premonitions. My mother was worried about me so she took me to see a witch doctor. No, that won't work. How about this: when I was young, I had a math tutor who had a unique way of teaching geometry and— no, that won't work either. Oh, just go ahead and tell her the truth, she's your wife for god's sake.

"Jesse, I don't know where to start. This could take all day…"

It didn't take all day. But almost. By early evening, I had told Jessica everything I remembered. I dredged up all kinds of stuff that had been buried for years. I told her about the fire dreams and premonitions and the guilt I'd carried all my life because of it. I told her about my mother's concerns. I told her about the priest. I told her about Ava. I told her about the day at the cemetery. I told her about my memories of my family. And finally, I told her about the strange symbols. I asked her if she thought it was crazy. I asked her if she thought it made any sense at all. I asked her if she thought it was strange.

We cried, and laughed, and cried some more. Jessica listened and told me about some of her own painful childhood memories. Doesn't everyone have them, she asked. And yet, in spite of my initial concerns, and much to my surprise, she was empathetic and understanding. By the end of the night, she said she thought some of what I told her was odd, but then continued, "I think you should try to get in touch with this woman. I think you should get the package too."

"Are you serious?" I asked.

She took both of my hands in hers. "Why not, what do you have to lose? It sounds like this woman is just trying to help you. You don't have to believe everything she's told you. You don't have to buy her story about your destiny, and all that stuff, but obviously she's trying to give you a gift. I think it's sweet, and it's a connection to your childhood. You should go, honey."

That night, with the kids farmed out for the weekend with the neighbors or school friends, Jessica and I drank wine and listened to music and talked to each other in a way we hadn't done since that summer we first met. We fell asleep in each other's arms, on the floor, in front of the fire.

I dreamed of Ava that night. And in my dream, she was a young woman. She was unpacking boxes as she moved into a Spanish colonial house, with an exquisite garden, a fabulous water fountain, and lush, colorful flowers and plants.

I woke up refreshed and told Jessica I would try to get in touch with Ava.

1996

I sent two letters to the return address on Ava's letter. Several months passed and both of my letters were returned, marked "UNDELIVERABLE." I tried unsuccessfully for another month or so to get in touch with her.

When it became clear that any further attempts would more than likely be fruitless, and after some encouragement from Jessica, I made plans to fly up to my old hometown and try to find the package. I didn't want anyone to know I was coming in. It was going to be a stealth trip: I would fly up, rent a car, drive to the white house with black shutters, if it was still there, and make my way down the path to the cabin where Ava once lived.

I landed at the airport on a cloudy, drizzly, downright ugly, gray day, in early February, and drove a couple of hours to my destination. The white house with the black shutters was still there. It was run down since I had last been there, so much so, that it looked like it could be abandoned. I didn't think anybody lived there.

Large sections of cracked white paint peeled away from the house like dead skin. Most of the shutters, grayed and speckled from the wind and rain and snow, hung lop-sided from their hinges. Several shutters barely clung to the faded, white wooden frame.

Slinging my back-pack with a short gardener's shovel inside over one shoulder, I made my way up the front steps and knocked several times on the door. When it seemed no one would answer, I decided to walk the path to Ava's cabin. I passed the wooden gate that marked the entrance to the trail.

The path was familiar. Where did the time go? Nothing had changed, or so it seemed. So I walked past the familiar trees and rocks to Ava's cloistered haven.

When I arrived at her cabin it looked like it had been preserved in a solution which rendered it changeless. Had someone kept up the place? Was Ava still living here? Should I knock on the door?

I knocked. No one answered. I knocked again, still no answer. I turned the door handle and walked inside. The kitchen table where we used to have our lessons was still there in the same spot. Had Ava been here recently? How could it be that so little had changed? That was thirty years ago. I looked around quickly, and then walked outside.

The rose trellis was still there, too, just like it had been many years ago. Gone now, though, were the robin's nest and any sign of the birds that made it their home. Green ivy had grown over the window panes that used to be bare. There, on the ground in the matted grass, beside the oak tree, was a small stone cross.

I took my shovel from my back-pack and dug into the damp, moist ground. A foot down, my shovel struck something hard. I dug faster, throwing scoops of dirt into a pile around where I dug. With each shovelful of dirt, my heart beat faster. I dug and scraped and clawed at a hard metal box. I pulled the box out and brushed off the dirt.

I stuck the box in my pack-pack, refilled the hole, and stood there wondering what to do next. I looked up into the sky. I took a deep breath. I walked inside and sat at the table. I set the box on the table and opened it. Inside was a large envelope wrapped in air-tight plastic wrap.

I took out my pocket knife and cut the plastic carefully, so as not to damage what I expected to find inside. I opened the package. Inside the envelope were three, thick, white papers with a symbol on each paper; and several notebooks filled with Ava's elaborate notes and drawings, and formulas and instructions. I placed the papers and instructions back in the envelope and put the metal box back inside my backpack then closed the door and walked back to my car.

My heart was still pounding hard as I passed the house. Just as I reached the gate I heard a noise. A door slammed. An old woman stepped out onto the porch.

"Hey mister, what do you think you're doing on my property?"

I took a step toward the porch. "Hello there," I called out. "I'm sorry. I hope I didn't scare you. I knocked on the door several times, but when no one answered I went down the path to see a woman who lived near the river."

With the help of a crooked brown cane, the old woman hobbled toward the front porch steps. She leaned on the cane. "Nobody lives down there no more. How'd you know there was something down there anyway?"

I walked closer to the steps. "You're Martha, right? Do you remember me?" I asked. "I used to come here when I was a boy to see a woman named Ava."

The old woman smiled. "You're that boy?" She laughed, "Why, you're all grown up, now!"

I stepped onto the first step. "Yes, that happens," I said. "It was a long time ago. Do you know how I can find Ava? I got a letter from her a few months ago and I'd like to get in touch with her."

The woman moved a little closer to the edge of the porch. "Why, Ava passed away a few months back," she said.

~

Jessica didn't ask much about my trip. Perhaps she knew I wanted to keep most of the memories to myself. She gave me space. We had gotten better about that as we got older.

I was reluctant at first to look at the contents of the package again. I kept it in my bedroom under a stack of books I hadn't bothered with in years. Then after a couple days when I was alone in the house, I opened the package and looked.

I opened one of the books marked Time Portals. Inside were elegant, detailed, drawings of planets, and solar systems, and galaxies, all with precise measurements and diagrams of dimensions and realms of existence. How did she do this? What did it mean? What was she trying to show me? I rifled through the other notebooks awed by the scope and breadth of her work.

In spite of the complex drawing and words, her instructions seemed simple enough: Meditate on each of the three symbols daily, keep a journal of vivid dreams, do not assign any mental meaning to the images.

Why not? I thought. What do I have to lose? What could happen? Jessica was right. I didn't have to buy her story. But I could certainly try it on. So I followed Ava's instructions: I started my daily routine of sitting quietly and focusing separately on each of the three symbols for about five minutes each.

Days turned into weeks and weeks turned into months. After the first week I noticed an enhancement of my mood and my ability to concentrate. I felt better. After the first month I noticed that things seemed to work better. My life improved. Things seemed to flow and work out effortlessly. Three months passed. I grew more confident and found I no longer had an inner urge to judge. I was more willing to observe events and let them unfold without feeling like I had to take control. This was something new for me and I reveled in my new-found well being. I thought about that time that Ava had given me the first symbol and I remembered how I felt after the first few weeks.

I dreamed some dreams but nothing exceptionally vivid. I continued to feel better emotionally. The sense of calm and grace I experienced grew more profound each month. I wondered how long this enhanced state would last. Without thinking much about it, I cut down on my drinking significantly, to the point where I only occasionally had a glass of wine with dinner. After several more months, I dreamed some dreams but recorded only a few in my journal.

Then one night I had a dream:

I'm standing in the river behind my house with Maria. The water is shallow, up to our knees. She and I are scooping old-fashioned baby dolls out of the water: the kind with eyelids that close when you tilt the head back. We scoop up dozens of dolls and place them in a white sack. It's a bright sunny day but the water is murky and brown.

I reach into the water and I scoop up a doll and realize that it's actually a dead baby. The baby is Maria's daughter. I walk to Maria and hold out the baby. Maria takes the baby in her arms and begins to cry. I tell her not to worry because something wonderful is going to happen. She looks at the baby. Then, the baby comes back to life. Maria smiles.

Maria sets her baby down in the water. The baby becomes a child. Maria and her child walk out of the river together, over the riverbank, and in the direction of the setting sun.

～

I woke up around three. I was on my knees in the middle of the bed. And for a few moments, even though the room was dark, and only a little light from the moon filtered in through the windows, I could see everything clearly as if it was the middle of the afternoon. I knelt in the bed in a daze trying to snap myself out of a fog.

Jessica awakened and calmed me and told me it was only a dream and comforted me back to sleep. I told Jessica about the dream over a cup of coffee that morning. She asked me what I thought it meant. I told her I had no idea but that I hadn't dreamt like that in a long time. It reminded me of the kind of dreams I used to have when I was a kid. Jessica asked if I wrote the dream in my journal. I told her I did.

The subject changed, with neither of us giving the dream much more thought. We talked about the kids and what was going on for the weekend. Then, around nine, just as I was getting ready to walk out the door for the office, the phone rang.

Jessica answered. "Hold on one minute. He's right here," she said. She handed me the phone. "It's your cousin Carol," she whispered.

"Oh, really? Great! I haven't heard from her in a while." I put the phone to my ear. "Hello, Carry. What's goin' on?"

I could hear her take a deep breath.

"Joe, I just wanted to call to let you know. If you haven't already heard, Maria Fedderson passed away last night."

"You've got to be kidding me," I said.

"No," she said. "It's a real shock. Apparently, she died in her sleep. Mark tried to wake her but she was already gone. They think it was an aneurism or something. She's your age, isn't she? Young."

"But why...how..." I stuttered.

"Oh, Joe. That's what we all thought," Carol said. "Do you think you can make it up?"

"Carol, no — I..."

"Oh it's okay. I know you're busy, but I thought you might want to send Mark a card or something. He sure has had a string of bad luck. First his daughter. Now Maria."

I held the phone to my ear and looked at Jessica. Carol was silent for a moment. Then she spoke again. "Oh, and you might want to get in touch with Albert," she said. "He's really been struggling lately. I saw him last week at a family picnic. He's lost weight. He didn't look so good. We think he's using drugs."

"He's probably been using them for awhile," I said.

"I don't know," Carry said. "Maybe you're right. He asked about you. I think he really misses you, Joe."

She waited for my answer, but I didn't have one. An image started to form: Albert reeling, falling...but I pushed it away. Then Carry spoke again. "Hey, I'm sorry about Maria. I know you two were close once. Joe, I gotta go. I'll call you in a couple of days, okay? We miss you. Come home and visit soon, okay?"

I hung up the phone.

"Got to be kidding about what?" Jessica asked.

"Maria Fedderson died in her sleep last night."

"Oh, my god! Your dream last night!" Jessica said.

I flopped into a chair. "Yes. The dream. And Ava's package."

"Do you think it had anything to do with those drawings you've been looking at?" Jessica asked.

∼

Could it be that I had something to do with Maria's death? I put all the notebooks and folders and the symbols in a box. I put the dream journal away. I told myself that someday I should just burn the box with all the stuff in it.

Just burn it all. I had had enough of Ava's magic. I was done with it once and for all.

But I heard that little voice again. And it said, don't be afraid.

What was it about these symbols? Maybe they did give me access to other dimensions. And what would that mean? Is that what happened with my dream of Maria? Had I tapped into something?

That day, I thought about the times with Maria. I remembered when we were young, when life seemed so simple and uncomplicated. I remembered how we used to play when we were kids, and how she helped me deal with my sadness and despair after the loss of my family. And I remembered our first kiss. And I cried.

So once again my connection with Ava had ultimately brought only death. That night, I took out the bourbon and tied one on. And kept tying them on, night after night.

The Light Place

The whiteness is all around me again. Glowing. Shining. Shimmering.

Music whispers and sighs. Notes caress each cell, each corpuscle.

I'm falling, floating.

I'm dying.

"Joe." A woman's voice. A voice I know.

"Who's there?"

I hold up my hand to shield my eyes from the blinding light as crystals or diamonds or some kind of something I don't know what, cling to me.

"Look over here. Do you see me?"

"No! Help me, I'm falling. I can't see. It's too bright."

"Let go. Just surrender to it. You'll be okay. Let yourself fall. It's okay. Give yourself time to adjust to the light."

"I'm breaking apart. I'm blinking on and off. Where are you—oh, please, can you help?"

"Let go. Let the light absorb you. Let yourself fall."

"What's happening to me? I'm breaking apart. Am I dying?"

I grab my wrist to make sure it's still solid, to make sure I'm still here. But I'm nothing but a bundle of light.

"You're going to be okay. I'm here now. Can you see me?"

"I can see a little better now."

"Be calm. Look over here."

I turn my head toward the sound of her voice. Out of the light, a solid image forms. First indistinctly, then it takes the shape of a woman. Her eyes are golden-brown, her skin is a light olive, her hair is almost black, and it curls softly to her shoulders.

"Maria, is that you?"

"Yes, it's me. There's not much time. I learned you were here so I asked to see you. I don't have long. Listen to me Joe. Do you know what's happening to you?"

Maria's image fades in and out.

"I'm not sure. I think I'm dying. Is this part of it?"

"Yes, you're between life and death, Joe. And the time for your decision is drawing near. I can't stay long. I'm here to tell you that you can still go back."

"What do you mean?"

"It's not over yet. It's not too late. You can still go back."

The light fades to a pallor of lavender and orange and pink and suddenly the free fall stops. I'm on solid ground. I try to stand.

I'm sitting on the bench, next to the brook, in the twilight. Maria sits next to me. Soft thick snowflakes land around us. The cottage windows glow from just across the stone bridge where now a snowman holds a broom.

"Is this what it's like to die?"

Maria slides close to me and puts her hand in mine. "For you it is," she says. "Everyone's experience is different. Everyone leaves Earth in a unique way. But everyone leaves at some point, Joe."

"What was it like for you?"

"It was easy for me. I died in my sleep." She looks at me. "You didn't have to suffer to come here, Joe. You had a choice."

I squeeze her hand. "I'm beginning to understand that now," I say. "I dreamed of you the night you died, didn't I?"

"Yes, you did. You're the one who helped me. It could have been someone else with the light, but it was you. I'm here to thank you. It wasn't the symbols, Joe. I know you thought that at the time. The symbols were a part of it. But only a small part—it was what they represent.

"When Ava taught you to meditate she taught you how to quiet your mind and tap into the stillness—the higher mind. Then, when you learned about the three symbols and used them in meditation, you awakened.

"This may be hard for you to understand right now, but it's important Joe. If you go back don't be afraid. Don't be afraid of living in an awakened state. And don't be afraid to listen to the inner voice."

"You know about Ava."

Maria smiles and looks at me. "Yes, of course, we all know Ava here."

"The woman I met when I arrived?"

Maria smiles again. "Yes."

"I knew it! I knew that was Ava."

Maria moves closer to me, and places her head on my shoulder without saying a word and rests it there for a little while. Then she sits up straight and looks at me again. "There's so much to tell you Joe. But my time here is short."

She peers up into the falling snow and takes a deep breath. She glances at me and her face shines with light.

"I came to this place in that dream, Joe. I had a chance to see my life in a new way. All my friends, and relatives, those who had gone before me, gathered for a celebration in my honor. My little girl was there. My little lost baby girl. This is what I had prayed for every night: that I could see her again. Hold her — again." Maria's eyes fill with tears.

I put my hand on the back of her neck, just where it joins her shoulders. "Oh Maria, I'm so sorry that happened. If anything ever happened to one of my…"

"It's okay," she interrupts. "I know now that it's okay, although it nearly destroyed me at the time. I see now that I was given exactly what I needed. Amazing things happen here, Joe. She's all healed now, and whole again — a beautiful little girl."

She rests her hand on my leg. I look down. Her hand seems to pass through me as if I am nothing more than air. "They're preparing a celebration for you," she says.

Maria continues. "Joe, at one point during the celebration, a woman offered me a bottle. I think the woman was Ava. I thought it was a bottle of wine. But it was something else — a powerful elixir. When she handed me the bottle, everything stopped. I opened it and the most fragrant aroma filled the room: the smell of peaches and cherries and strawberries and almonds. I knew if I drank from the bottle, I would stay here and be with my daughter again."

I reach to touch her face and my hand passes through her cheek, trailing sparks of colored light behind it.

"It was a difficult decision," she says. "But I was heartbroken after my daughter died. She was our only child, and she died too young. Joe, after her death, I felt like a part of me died with her. Oh, I knew Mark would be sad, but I knew he was strong enough to go on without me. And I wanted to be with my daughter again. Look around you, Joe. Look at the light and the colors glistening off the snow. Look at the beauty. Have you ever felt peace like this? We all have to leave the Earth sometime, Joe. It was my time."

"So, is this place heaven?"

Maria smiles. "I guess you can say it's some kind of heaven—but no more than the heaven you can have on Earth, Joe. Everyone makes their own heaven, or hell for that matter, one way or another."

"So you drank from the bottle?"

"Oh yes, I drank, and the nectar tasted so sweet and pure. It was the nectar of everlasting life. As soon as I drank, the long thin cord that connected my heart to Earth snapped. When that happened, I knew I wasn't going back again. I had made my decision. My physical body died. It was painless.

"On Earth, they said it was an aneurism. I heard them talking about it there. Did you hear static when you first arrived here Joe? Well, I did. That was part of it I guess. And I saw them standing over my body and trying to revive me. But I didn't feel a thing, just the snap of the cord. And then I was here. I think I died of a broken heart Joe. It just stopped beating.

"You helped me. After the cord snapped, I was in the water with you. Remember your dream? You put my daughter in my arms and she came back to life. Remember? And then we walked out of the water together. Then I was with my daughter, here in this place."

Maria looks up into the pink light. "No one ever really dies, Joe. It just seems that way on Earth. It's passing from one realm into another."

As Maria speaks, a soft, delicate hum rises and floats effortlessly in the ether: a soft harmonic resonance — an oboe, a violin, a harpsichord, notes and sounds, drifting and lingering.

"Ava was trying to give you a gift," she says. "A gift of higher consciousness — an awareness of being pure light and love. Ava was trying to show you how to tap into that — how to tap into the kind of love that survives everything."

Maria is changing. She is a panorama of light and fire. Radiant and sublime. Her form is barely perceptible, and yet, undeniably present. And now I sense her desire. An inexhaustible desire to keep her flame alive.

"My time is almost up," she says.

Is it the insight of dying that brings me the realization, or am I becoming more aware? I don't know. But in this moment I realize Maria has summoned every bit of her will to appear before me. "Wait, please stay," I say.

"I'm sorry Joe. I've already stayed too long." Maria's image flickers on and off. But she persists. And her image stabilizes faintly. "Oh Joe, remember how we used to play? Remember our first kiss? We were just children then. But children grow up and confront the harsh reality of the world, don't they? Your world changed after the fire at your house, Joe. I was so sad for you. But you were strong. You persevered. You pushed ahead so valiantly. I knew you would make it in the world and be a success. But I always believed you would be a force for good and spend your talents on things that really matter."

I reach for Maria's hand. When I touch her hand the colored light sparkles around it. "Maria, tell me what really matters."

Maria caresses my cheek. Softly. Gently. "You'll have to learn that for yourself Joe. I can only tell you what really mattered to me. What really mattered to me was that I opened my heart and gave love."

She kisses my lips.

"I love you Joe. It's time."

Maria's image dissolves to a blur of circles and lines and back again, slowly fading in and out. "One last thing, Joe," she says. "As beautiful and peaceful as it is here," she says, "If I could have my daughter with me, I would make the choice to live life on Earth again—it's such a gift."

Then there's a flash of light. And Maria appears in front of me perfectly clear one last time: her almond eyes, her olive skin, her hair curling softly to her shoulders, her lips pressed together in a soft smile.

I sit on the bench and watch her fade into the falling flakes of snow.

ALBERT

The news of Albert came rolling in like a thunderstorm over the Great Lakes.

I was lying in bed next to Jessica that night. I had just finished reading the first chapter of a new book. I had turned out the light, and was about to fall asleep, when the phone rang. I had my usual response to a ringing telephone at that hour of the night: a knock in the pit of my stomach, and then a tightening in my throat.

I reached for the phone. Who the hell is this, I thought. I knocked over the glass of water I almost always set on my bedside table to drink during the night, but usually didn't. Water spilled onto the floor.

"Ah shit. Hello."

"Joe."

"Yeah… Paul?" His voice sounded different: gruff and gravelly.

"I have some bad news. I hate to call you now so late, but." He cleared his throat. "But I didn't want to wait until morning."

"What's going on?"

A long pause. Paul cleared his throat again. "It's about Albert."

I pulled myself up and rested against the headboard. "What happened?" I knew what Paul was going to tell me but I didn't want to hear it.

"I don't how to tell you this." Paul's voice cracked and he started to cry. I heard whispers and a shuffling sound in the background and a woman's voice, hoarse and raspy. "Here Paul, give me the phone. Let me talk.

"Joe, this is Nancy. Albert was found dead late this afternoon outside his apartment. We're not sure what happened."

I sat up and turned on the light, squinted in the brightened room.

"The police are still there with the family," Nancy said. "Somebody said somebody heard a gunshot. But we just don't know yet. Paul's really upset. Everyone is."

Jessica rolled over and looked at me — a puzzled look on her face.

"Oh shit Nancy. Damn. Damn. I should have done something. I knew it."

Jessica sat up, dazed and startled. "What is it Joe?"

"It's Albert. He's dead."

THE LIGHT PLACE

Pink dissolves into grey. Tangerine and raspberry mix with the seraphic whiteness. Colors crisp and sharp. The snow falls hard. I sit on the bench and look at the cottages just beyond the stone bridge. I think about what Maria said. This is not a dream. This is real.

Crystal blue lights line the edges of the bridge. A woman carrying a small pot walks over it and vanishes into the curtain of snow.

A scatter of branches shakes behind me. I turn. Two forms emerge from a forest through the dense, falling snow, and make their way: a boy and a white dog. The boy sits near me on the bench with his dog at his feet. He loosens the orange scarf around his neck.

"It's you! You're here," I say.

"You didn't find me," the boy says.

The boy commands his dog to sit, and stay. He touches the dog's head gently and runs his hand over its fluffy white coat.

"You didn't find me and your time is up."

Here he is at last. How could I have possibly found him? If it is a game we're playing, then I have lost. Who is this child? Is he the reason I'm here? The woman said he had something for me. This might be my last chance.

"I know I didn't find you. But you found me. Do you have something for me?" I look at the boy. I can't help but notice what used to be my own body: my torso, my arms and legs, my hands and feet, now a bundle of white and violet and pink reticulating a human shape and form.

The boy looks at me and then turns and glances at the forest. He ignores my question. At least he's consistent. "The game is over," he says. Snow falls. Whiteness now blankets the misty sky. The boy looks back at the path and the forest again.

He says the game is over but does he want to keep playing?

"Is someone in there? Who's in there?" I ask.

The boy straightens. He commands his dog to jump. The dog jumps on the bench and sits. "My family," he says.

"Your family?"

I move my hand to touch his dog. The dog licks my open palm. The boy tightens the scarf around his neck and swings one end of it over his shoulder and looks up.

"They heal me," he says.

~

It's been snowing hard since the boy arrived. White flakes float to the ground in heaps and piles. I notice the snow weighing down the branches, how it has piled up on the bridge and covered the cottage rooftops. The lights in the cottages are barely visible through the snow. The blue lights lining the bridge are now just snow-covered domes. I see the faint glow of a lamplight and its reflection in the glossy surface of the dark blue stream. I watch the boy.

"The game is over. It's time to go," he says. He jumps from the bench.

"Wait. Where are you going?"

He taps his dog on the head and runs toward the bridge. The dog leaps behind him, leaving no tracks in the snow.

"Wait. Come back!" The snow falls hard. I can't see the little boy or his dog. I hear a faint call as he trails off into the billow. "It's Christmas!"

I sit for a moment. I look at myself, all violet and white and pink, meshed and mingled and woven. Then I jump up and run across the bridge. I open the cottage door. The boy sits in front of a fireplace with his dog.

He looks at me calmly, as if he expects me to follow him. He stands. His image and form begin to change. He looks at me. He changes to a young man and then back to a boy. The image shifts back and forth in waves. Finally, it becomes clearer and I can see it's a young man. It looks like Albert. He speaks muffled sounds that I cannot understand at first and then his form becomes stable.

"Albert, is that you?" I ask.

"I'm sorry Joe. I'm so sorry."

There's blood on his clothes and his face is scruffy and unshaven. He turns and shows me a wound in the back of his head.

"Oh Albert! So you're the little boy!"

"I'm sorry Joe. I'm sorry you had to be the one."

"Sorry for what?"

"For bringing you here."

I move closer to him. "You brought me here?"

"Yes, I called you. You came. I need you here."

"You called me here?"

"Yes"

"But how—what do you mean, you called me?"

"That night in the snow."

"You mean you were the child in the field?"

Albert, or whatever he is, steps toward me. Blood is caked on his neck and splattered across the front of his shirt; his clothes are tattered and torn. "Yes, in the field."

Albert steps again toward me, extending his blood-stained hand. I move away. "Albert, are you dying?"

"No, I already died. You're dying."

"But I'm not dead yet, am I?"

"Look at yourself."

"I know. I don't know what to make of it."

"You're close to the end now."

Albert tries to touch my hand.

"Don't be afraid. I can help you." His form vibrates in waves. Then he spins, rotating, faster and faster.

"Albert, what's happening?"

The spinning continues and then slows until I see him as something altogether different: a being of perfection, young and beautiful.

"Albert?"

"Yes it's me—me, as I really am."

"I know about the symbol," he continues. "I can show you something."

"You know…What are you talking about?"

"The fourth symbol—the symbol of awakening and immortality. Listen, there's not much time," he says. "I think you know what I'm talking about—your connection with Ava. She's been a part of my healing here. She understands the future of our world. Conflict and greed and negativity will destroy it. But it can be changed if enough people awaken. That's what Ava was trying to teach you. And there are others who have the knowledge and it's time for them to share it."

"Albert, what you're talking about—it's too big. No one can…"

"Joe, it's not too big. And there's hope. But the human mind in its identity with the ego can't understand it. The ego will destroy the earth. The ego is the illusion—not this. No, this—what you find here—this is not a dream or an illusion. This is the truth. This is a world of love and light. And it can be this way on Earth too. It can be heaven."

Albert continues. "I'm going to show you how I died so you'll know the truth," Albert says. "It was an accident." He changes from his perfect form to something awful: pathetic.

He wipes some blood from his face. He stands there gray and ashen. His cheeks smeared with dirt and grit.

"Albert? What's happening now?"

"This is the last time you will see me this way. I'm doing this for you, so you will understand what happened to me—I was an addict," he says.

I see now what it was I had tried to avoid. His life—the sadness and despair, the wretched condition Albert had lived in. I try to move toward him, to comfort him. "Did anybody know you were addicted?" I know my question is insincere. I knew. I knew.

"Just the ones who didn't care."

I flinch at his answer. "You could've called me. I might have been able to help. I could have sent money."

"Yes, I could have called, and you would've come, or you would have sent money, and you would have tried to stop me. Do you really think your money would have helped? I would have just used it to buy more junk. I didn't want to stop. And it wouldn't have helped. That's why I didn't call. But I called you here."

I look away. I don't want to see this.

"Look at me," he says.

"What about the family?"

"They tried to love me and take care of me. It wasn't their problem to fix. It wasn't their fault. They did the best they could. I know that now. I didn't mean to do it. Really I didn't. I didn't mean for it to happen. But I was messed up."

"The gunshot?"

"Went off when I hit the ground—a freak accident."

"The back of your head?"

"Not a pretty sight is it?—blew out the left-side of my brain. This is how I looked when I arrived here. But I won't be like this much longer."

I try to touch him. But he raises his hand as if to signal that he cannot be touched. "These wounds are almost healed now—remnants of memories and desires."

He's becoming a boy again, slowly, before my eyes.

"I went to church that day," he says. "I'm not sure why. I felt better for a while. It was icy cold, and the roads were slick, but it was a sunny day, and that cheered me up. But as the day wore on I became depressed. I was so tired. I tried to take a nap. There was too much noise in my head. I couldn't turn it off. I kept hearing voices and feeling the sadness. I just wanted it to stop. But it didn't.

"So I got up from my bed and walked to the closet. I put my hand in the old shoe box where I kept the gun and pulled it out. I looked at it. I sat on the bed. I took my little kit out of my dresser drawer. I spread a piece of aluminum foil on my lap and put a little mound of dust on it. I rolled a five dollar bill and put it in my mouth and made a flame underneath the foil. Then I lit it up from below and made sure to inhale all the fumes. It was as if my skull had been torn apart and all its contents mixed with the universe. I was so high. I walked down the stairs and opened the front door. I didn't see the ice on the steps."

He turns and gently pats the back of his head and shows me his hand. No more blood.

"Everything disappeared," he says. "I thought when I died I would see a light. I thought I would be greeted by friends or angels. But all I got was a black pool. And it was just black for a long, long, time. A hundred years, a thousand, maybe more. I don't know.

"Then I heard my mother crying. And I saw light. My mother was on her knees praying for me. She was all alone in her room. I heard her prayers and I came out of the black. A mother's love, Joe—the power of that kind of love survives everything, even death. Love and prayers, strong enough to pull me out of hell, the hell I created for myself on Earth.

"I went to her. The light got brighter. I was coming out of the darkness. I tried to put my arms around her. But she couldn't feel me and I couldn't feel her. I began to see more light. As I came out of the darkness, I saw people and things. I was there but I wasn't there.

"I wondered if I had ever left. I was looking at everything through a filter. I tried to talk to people because it was so real to me. After a time I realized I couldn't communicate with anyone. That was the strangest part of all—to be there next to someone, so close—and yet not there at all.

"So I wandered around with my hazy vision in a place between Earth and some other place. At first I was aware of everything that had happened. I saw people standing over my body. I saw them carry me away. And when I saw the pain I inflicted by my actions on the people who loved me, I began sinking again, down into the black pool."

If I have a face, it is wrenched in sorrow, if I have eyes they are crying. My Albert, my sweet cousin Albert.

"But then," Albert continued, "a pair of hands grabbed me under my arms. A pair of strong and gentle hands Joe, just like yours. Remember your dream? It was you who pulled me out of that black pool. And I was here in this place and the healing began, and I will become a child again. A little child whole and healthy."

Three symbols float between us: a circle with a solid dot in the center, a cross, and a triangle.

These are the three symbols Ava gave me. And now it all begins to make sense. The little boy knows about the symbols. He knew all along.

He lifts the symbols from the air and shapes them into one—a beautiful design that looks like a snowflake: just like the one he made in the cave. Then he holds the symbol over his heart. He holds it there for a moment then he pulls it into himself.

"You might have been able to help me, Joe," he says.

"With the symbols?" I ask.

"If you had listened to Ava you'd have understood what she was trying to do for you. You could have stayed in an awakened state. You were there for awhile. You might have helped me and others. Things might have been different. My life might have been changed. But you didn't trust it. You didn't open your heart."

Or maybe I did, I think. Maybe we all do what we must do. To a point. Maybe it's just that we miss the signs, because we let our desires get in the way. "Is that why I'm here?" I ask Albert.

"Yes," he says. "I called you here. I need you to be here, to awaken, and to tell me the story. Then my healing will be complete—and our rebirth."

"What story?"

"The story of our lives."

"But that could take days. I thought you said there's not much time."

He smiles. "With the angels anything is possible. With the angels it can happen in an instant. With the angels there is no time."

We're in front of the fireplace again. Have we been here all along? The dog is still sitting at our feet. I look at Albert — the little boy. "So that's why I'm here. It's for you, isn't it?"

Albert nods. "It's for both of us," he says. "I'm sorry Joe. I know it's a lot to ask. But it's the only way. It's up to you now, Joe. It's your choice."

"But why me?"

"Because you were the one who loved me the most."

Then, like seeing a car in the distance on a hot summer day when the heat is rising from the road, I watch the image of Albert as he becomes younger and younger. When he speaks again he's a child. His golden hair shines. And close to his heart, the symbol: a crystalline snowflake, encompassed in an emerald flame, the essence of his existence. I know he is about to leave. But too much is left unsaid. Too much is unexplained. "Albert, wait! Don't go yet. I have to know."

"Our time is over now," he says.

"What about the fourth symbol? Where is it?"

The child moves his hands to his chest, and covers his heart. Then he raises his hand. A signal that what's done is done. There will be no more. He opens the door and it's morning and the snow has stopped and the sun is shining and everything glistens in white. He points to a cottage in the forest across the bridge.

"Over there," he whispers. "Remember, with the angels anything is possible."

He taps my hand. I kneel in front of him so I can look in his eyes. He kisses my cheek. I reach to hug him. But before I can, he disappears.

The Celebration

I'm floating over hills and valleys. I see my reflection in a rainbow. The wind whispers my name. Echoes and voices surround me. I'm falling through a field of snowflakes that look like blossoms blown in the springtime breeze: pink snowflakes like cherry blossoms, white like dogwood blossoms, yellow like jasmine.

A voice.

A light.

Welcome home Joe.

I know that voice. Danny? Eagle Eyes is that you? Is it really you?

"It's me, Joe. It's really me. And I have new eyes. I can see you. Come to the light."

Am I dying?

"Don't be afraid, Joe."

Scenes from my childhood, from my adult life, spread out before me. Is life a dream? A memory?

I hear another voice: "Fall into my arms."

Mom?

And another voice: "Come this way, you're almost home."

Dad?

Oh, the light!

~

I float into a room full of tables covered in white linen. Rows of tables set with fine bone china, and gold-lined silver goblets.

A shiny blue floor, deep, deep, indigo blue, almost black, punctuated with streaks of golden light, stretches to where the tables end. And beyond that, the light stretches forever, beyond the edges of the universe, beyond the edges of time, until a billion stars shine in the midnight sky.

A bell. A woman in white. She rings the bell. "It has begun!"

A cheer!

And then quiet. My mother and father and my three brothers stand before me, in front of the first row of tables.

My father wears a black tuxedo with a white bow tie. His thick, dark hair is perfectly groomed, neat and wavy. He's in his mid-twenties and looks like he does in the old wedding picture that hangs in the hallway of my home.

My mother holds a bouquet of red roses against her white wedding gown. Her ruby lips part ever so slightly in a smile. She, too, is in her mid-twenties and looks like the woman in the wedding picture.

My brothers are dressed in dinner jackets and black bow ties. Each as they would have looked had they lived. Each the age they were at the time of the fire. As if they had been waiting for me.

Jake, the oldest, still tall and slender, still the athlete, stands before me, smiling. He brushes his fine, light brown hair from where it falls, just above his eyebrows that accentuate his gleaming blue eyes.

James stands next to him. He's shorter than Jake. He lifts both arms and beckons to me, just like he did when I was a little boy.

And my brother Michael with his curly auburn hair and round nose is the shortest. He's squat and muscular. He smiles that big toothy smile of his — the one that always made my heart light up.

In an instant, I see what was, what is, and what might have been.

Michael steps forward and takes my hand. "Come with me," he says.

It's summertime and I'm running along the beach at North Shore Park trailing behind Michael and my two older brothers. A warm breeze blows and waves crash into the shoreline. The sun is a bright orange ball just about to drop into the water. Above the horizon, over the lake, the sky is colored golden-peach. I'm five years old. Michael is eight. James is ten. Jake is thirteen.

James has the kite and he's running up a sand dune. Michael and John are running with him. I'm running as fast as I can but I can't keep up.

"Come on Joe," Jake yells.

But I can't run as fast as my brothers. They run up and over the sand dune and I can't see them anymore. I fall down and scrape my knee on a rock that had been covered by the sand. I lie in the sand and cry. I see the kite's tail dancing in the wind, but then it disappears. No one else is around.

They've left me. It's getting dark and I don't know how to get back home. I'm scared. I lie in the sand and cry.

Then I see Jake. He's running toward me. He reaches me and kneels down. "Hey little buddy, what happened? Did you fall and hurt your knee?"

I'm crying. "I couldn't keep up. I thought you left me."

"Oh, I would never leave you," Jake says. "It's okay. You're a big boy now. You can keep up with us. You just fell and hurt your knee. I've fallen down plenty of times. But when I fall I try to get back up right away. That's what you have to do. Everybody falls down some time. The bad guys stay down, but the good guys get back up as soon as they can. You're a good guy, right?"

I nod my head, yes. I smile and stop crying. James and Michael are with us now and they're helping me up. Jake lifts me onto his shoulders and carries me. James and Michael cheer and clap. And I feel so much love. The kind of love I had forgotten.

Then I'm back in the room looking at my family. I hear the other people in the room talking and laughing but I can't see them. All I see is my family.

If I have breath, I cannot breathe. If I have a heart, it does not beat. If I have eyes, they do not see. My joy overflows. I have longed for this moment. Dreamed of it. Wished for it. I've missed them so much and now they're here.

James steps forward. He touches my arm.

It's a week or so before the fire at our house. I'm twelve. James is seventeen. It's Saturday night and James is going out on date with a girl. I'm in James's bedroom watching him get ready to go out.

"Are you going to make out with her at the movie?" I ask.

James makes a fist like he's going to punch me. Then he laughs. "What do you know about that? I see you've been hanging around with that girl Maria a lot these days," he says. "Is she your girlfriend?"

"No, she's just my friend," I say.

Mother opens the door and peeks in. "You better hurry James or you'll be late."

James looks in the mirror and combs his hair.

"Hey James," I say. "Are we still going fishing on Friday?"

"Sure—as soon as I get back from Dad's office. He's going to show me how to work that new X-ray machine. I'm going to go to school to be a doctor just like him."

I see James as a man in his early thirties. He's a doctor in our small town. He has a wife and two kids. I see his whole life stretched out before me. He sees it too. This is what I took away from him when I caused the fire.

"I'm so sorry James. I didn't mean to do it. It was an accident."

James smiles at me and then we're back in the crowded room. And I hear the people talking again.

I see aunts and uncles, cousins and friends, relatives far too many to count. Grandmothers, grandfathers, great-grandmothers and great-grandfathers, and on and on from a stream of infinite lifetimes: all who have gone before, and those yet to come, spread out before me: ripples in an endless stream.

A man with thick, dark red hair holds a bottle in his hand. It's old Uncle Lou, but he's young and vibrant now, in his late twenties. Yes, I remember this: his broad muscular shoulders, rugged face with high cheekbones, and a barely perceptible dimple in the center of his chin.

With one quick tug, he pulls the cork from the bottle with a loud pop. Bubbles spill out and float through the room. Another loud cheer, then laughter.

Uncle Lou makes an announcement, "Tonight someone has come home. Let us welcome him, everyone." Uncle Lou raises his glass and looks at me, "I propose a toast to Christmas Eve—the Feast of Light, and to Joe St. John, who is home at last."

Glasses clang. The sound vibrates throughout the room: a gentle hum that builds to a crescendo, with yet another volley of cheers.

I recognize people I have not seen in years: a cousin who died when I was just a child, a distant cousin killed in the Vietnam War, an uncle I hardly knew, but I remember him here and I know his life like I have known him forever. I know everyone in the room, all of these people returned to the youth that was, or might have been.

A young woman with curly black hair raises her glass and calls out, "Isn't this a wonderful party?"

Waiters in white tuxedos balance silver trays of food and drinks. Musicians with saxophones, trombones, and trumpets play songs from America's big-band era. The music wails in the background as people talk, dance, eat, or stroll from table to table.

Uncle Lou stands with his hands on his hips, surveying the family scene. Then he raises a hand high above his head, palm facing out, and says, "Hey Joe, not bad for a bunch of poor folks, huh?" Not bad for a bunch of poor folks. He'd always said that—at Christmas, at Easter, the Fourth of July, at any celebration where the tables were groaning with food, and we were sure we had all there was of the good life.

~

The room is quiet. My father steps forward and takes my hand. I'm seven years old. It's the day after one of my scary dreams.

My dad and I are outside in the fresh fallen snow. We're walking through the woods behind our house. The sun is shining and the sky is blue and the fresh fallen snow is pure white.

Daddy and I built a bunny rabbit trap a few weeks before, after I saw the bunny and told him I wanted to catch it. The trap looks more like a cage than a trap. We made it out of some wood scraps and wire mesh, with a little trap door. Daddy let me pound the nails into the wood with his hammer. We're walking to check the trap to see if we caught the bunny. This is the fourth time we've checked but we haven't seen any sign of it yet.

"Are you sure you saw a bunny out here?" Daddy asks as we walk through the snow.

"I saw it Daddy," I say. "It was right over there by that tree."

I point to an opening in the snow beneath an old oak tree. Daddy is playing along. I know he doesn't expect to catch the bunny, but he pretends. But as we approach the trap we see something small and brown and quivering inside.

I pull at my daddy's arm. "Look! There's something in the trap."

"Well, how about that. I think there is," he says. He scratches his head underneath his old earmuff hat.

"I told you! I told you! Look, there it is—just like I said. The trap worked. We caught him!"

Daddy is surprised. I run to the trap and Daddy walks close behind me. When we get there, he bends down and looks inside. "Well Joey, it looks like you caught a bunny." He sits on his haunches next to the trap and gently runs his hand across the wire mesh. I squat next to him.

"Can we take him home?"

Daddy looks at the bunny. It twitches, and its brown eyes blink. The bunny is trapped and I know it's afraid.

Daddy puts his hand on my shoulder. "Is that what you want to do?"

I look at the bunny. I get real close and look at its brown fur and fluffy tail. It looks so helpless and scared. But he's so cute and furry. I could talk to him, and feed him carrots. Maybe he would even let me hold him after awhile. I look straight into Daddy's face. "Yes," I say. "I want to take him home and keep him for a pet."

Daddy doesn't say anything right away, like he's thinking about something. "Okay then, let's take him home." Daddy picks up the cage and we head back through the snow. But after we walk a little ways, Daddy stops. He sets the trap on the ground. He looks at me then he looks at the bunny. "You know Joey," he says. "I think this is a baby bunny and it might be part of a family." Daddy touches the little trap door. "That means he might have brothers and sisters and a mommy and daddy. What do you think his family will do if he doesn't come home?"

I look at the bunny, my face close to the cage. The bunny flinches and curls up into a ball in one corner of the trap. It's shaking now—rapid, jerky little shakes.

"They'll be sad," I say. "They'll wonder what happened to him." The bunny buries his head under his front paws as if he's trying to hide. "They might try to find him." I say.

"Yes, I think they will."

"And the bunny will be sad because he won't be with his family anymore?"

"I think so."

I don't know what to do. I'm thinking real hard and Daddy puts his hands in his pockets.

"You don't have to take the bunny home," he says. "You can open the cage. He'll go back to his family."

I look at the bunny and then at Daddy. I think about it for a while. I'm torn. I want the bunny for a pet, but now I'm sad. I don't want the bunny to be without his family. I don't want the bunny to be lonely.

Daddy looks at the bunny. Then he looks at me. "It's up to you Joey," he says.

I kind of want to cry. I really do want that bunny. "I don't know Daddy, what do you think I should do?"

Daddy kneels on the ground and takes my hand. "Joey, sometimes it's hard to let go of the things we think we want. But sometimes we have to do that to do what's best for others and make room for something better for ourselves.

I know you really wanted to catch this bunny. So, I'm going to let you decide. It's up to you."

Daddy doesn't say another word. I wait for him to tell me what he thinks I should do but he doesn't. He just looks at me and waits.

I look at the bunny and he looks back at me—blinking slowly now and still shaking—resigned to its fate. And in that moment it seems as if I'm trapped inside that cage with the bunny and tears well up in my eyes and I look at Daddy and I say, "I think we should let him go."

Daddy smiles and asks me if I want to open the cage and I do and I swear that bunny looks at me and smiles. He hops out of the cage and bounces his way back to the hole in the snow, and a week later, just before Christmas, Daddy brings home the new puppy I name Paddy.

Then I'm back at the celebration again.

THE CHOICE

My father lets go of my hand. And I see his life stretched out before me—the life that would have been had he lived. I see him receiving honors and awards. I see the good work he does for our small town and the community. I see him as a grandfather playing with my children.

I know now what I lost out on by not having him around. Not having him around to talk to when I needed advice. His wisdom. His mentoring. I lost out on the man who would have been my best friend.

I look at him standing there next to my mother and my brothers. "I'm so sorry," I say. "I'm so sorry for disobeying you. I didn't mean to leave the lantern on the table. I didn't mean to cause the fire."

I've fallen to my knees on the floor and I'm crying. My mother kneels and wraps her arms around me. "What do you mean, Joey? What lantern are you talking about?" she asks.

My head is on her shoulder and tears flow down my cheeks. "Daddy's lantern in the basement—the one I left burning before I left for Albert's birthday party. The one the dog knocked over. The one that caused the fire."

Mother cradles my face in her hands and looks deeply into my eyes. "Who told you it was you who caused the fire," she asks.

I'm still crying. "That thing in the cave. That shadow thing," I sob.

Mother looks at my father. "No Joey. No. That's not what happened." She gestures for my father to join us. "Tell him, Jack." My mother reaches for my father's hand as he kneels beside me.

"No, Joe. The shadow lied to you," he says. "I put out the flame in the lantern. I walked downstairs after you left for Albert's party and saw it and I turned it out. That's not what caused the fire.

"Faulty wiring caused the fire. If anyone is to be blamed for the fire it's me. I helped build our house. I helped install the wiring. I thought I smelled smoke that night before I got in bed. But I dismissed it. I didn't go check on it."

My father hugs me. "The shadow lied to you," he says, "It will lie to you and try to deceive you. But it doesn't have to be that way. The shadow just wants to be seen, to be acknowledged, to be accepted. And then, when you can look at the dark places inside and see them for what they really are, you might find that there's a gift for you. And in that way, your shadow will serve you. And help you know what is true."

I hear the joyous laughter in the room again.

A woman emerges from the crowd. She looks like the woman I used to call the angel: the woman from my dreams. It's the woman who greeted me when I arrived here, when I climbed out of the snow cave.

And I know it's Ava.

She walks toward me and stands next to me and holds up a bottle just like Maria said she would. And everything stops. She looks into my eyes. The light—oh, the light is blinding! I try to look away but I cannot. I am drawn into the center of her eyes.

Inside her eyes I see numbers, letters, symbols, and alphabets, memories of every spoken language in the history of the universe. I see planets, moons, and stars: in a synchronized dance of rhythm and movement. Galaxies turn in an ever expanding flow of creation. New stars are born and old ones die, and as each star dies, dozens more burst into existence.

The planet Earth, a blue-green orb, floats in space, and men and women live on it. People sicken and die. I see mushroom clouds from nuclear explosions, I see birthday celebrations, I see fireworks on the Fourth of July. I see men going to war, and women giving birth.

I see the first morning of creation, chaotic, yet ordered and systematic. I see the landscapes of planets beyond Earth: lush and bountiful, teaming with new life. And I see death.

Ava offers me the bottle.

I know, rather than see, that a thousand eyes rest on me.

If I stay here, if I drink, I can be with my mother and father and my brothers again.

But what about Jessica? What about our children? And what about Albert?

I take the bottle from Ava's hand. I see my life on Earth.

The snowstorm is over. It's morning. The sun is shining. The snow is brilliant white. Paul and Caryn and John and Thomas and a group of men trudge through the railroad yard field where I fell into the snow cave. An ambulance and an emergency medical vehicle are in the nearby street, their lights flashing. I see myself unconscious in the snow cave.

Caryn sees something in the snow — a little mound that looks out of place. She digs at it. "His gloves!" she yells. "His hat, too! He must be close."

I lift the bottle. I think about Jessica and my children and I feel the pain and the cold. I pull the cork. Oh, the fragrance!

I think in this moment if I drink from the bottle I will leave my body in the snow and the pain and suffering will end. For a moment I don't want to go back to my life on Earth. I don't want to try anymore. I don't want to struggle with my shadow self, my sadness, my compulsions, my loss. I want the freedom and peace and love of this place. I want to be with my mother and father and my brothers again.

I look at all the faces in the room. I am truly home. And then I see Albert. And I know what I must do.

I raise the bottle to my lips.

~

"Over here," someone yells. "He's over here." It's Paul. Two men run through the snow with a stretcher.

Love, acceptance, and forgiveness are written on the faces in the room. My mother and father and my brothers look at me. I tilt my head back and lift the bottle. A drop of its nectar touches my lips and flows over my tongue.

Oh, the light!

And in this moment I understand the meaning of all existence and of my own. I understand the interconnectivity of everyone and everything. I sense the limitlessness and wonder of life. I know that I am a powerful, creative being. And yet, I also know that I am helpless and powerless. Ecstasy and awe engulf me and I have no comprehension of space or time.

I know now what Walt meant when he spoke of living with an open heart. I see my own life spread out before me, reordered and reprioritized. I see what it would be like to live with my new understanding and awareness. I see what it would be like to live from a place of inspiration and meaning. I see the positive impact I could have on my family, and all the lives I could inspire.

Then I hear Jessica's voice:

"Find the opening in heaven Joe — please come back to us."

And then Ava says to me:

"You have fulfilled your destiny here. Go back. It's not your time."

I choke. The bottle slips from my hand. It hits the ground and shatters.

Then each person in the room becomes a crystal snowflake: each one a unique, perfected, geometric design. The crystals spin into the shape of a funnel. Wind blows and voices sing. And then I'm pulled into the undulating funnel and I blend with the crystals into a kaleidoscope of color.

The crystalline funnel folds into itself and becomes a ball of violet-white. Every one of us, souls together, encapsulated in that light. And the ball becomes a beacon. And the beacon collapses, and launches us into boundless space, leaving a trail of sparkling adornment. Each soul, a brilliant white star.

I feel a hard tug then a gentle pull. I see a silver cord extending from the furthest reaches of heaven.

Flashing red lights.

Caryn screams, "Over here. Over here! Quick, he's over here!"

The rescue team pulls me from the snow cave. They lay me on a stretcher. My body is cold. So cold.

And all I see is white.

WITH THE ANGELS

The soft pink glow of dusk descends and the child is getting sleepy. His little head rests on my lap and he looks up at me with emerald eyes.

Is that the end of the story? He asks.

Yes, we've come to the end and now it's time for us to go to sleep. And when we awaken our new journey will begin.

Did the man in the story find the fourth symbol?

I believe he did. What do you think?

Yes, and I think Albert has it too.

You might be right.

What about the people of Earth? Will enough of them wake-up?

I don't know. What do you think?

I think they will.

I hope so. Time will tell.

And what happened to the little boy with the golden hair?

Well, he talked about rebirth.

Do you think that will happen?

Yes, I think it will.

What do you think he will do with the symbol?

I don't know Albert. It's up to you. Let's go to sleep now.

Acknowledgments

I would like to thank my wife Mary, and my sons Joe and Jack, whose boundless love, laughter, and friendship, inspire me and light my way.

I would also like to thank Benjie Nelson for her creativity and design; John and Barbara Hale for bringing clarity to the title; and Joseph Dispenza for his wise counsel—introducing me to "my inner voice" many years ago—and encouraging me to write this book.

For their support, encouragement, and generosity, I would like to thank my Aunt Anna and my Aunt Loretta, Bill and Kathy Savarise; Dave and Mary Jo Savarese; Al and Jan Guerini; Olympia Valentic, Lorenzo and Toni Carlisle—especially for the Eskimo proverb; Michael Herbert, Beverly Nelson, Laura Lowell, Jill Drinkwater, Stephanie Breslin, Skye Wentworth, Ray Arata, Gary Rosenberg, Stephan McLaughlin, Dan Dwyer, Scott Corbett, Al Boutin, Les Falke, Wendell Johnson, Bobby Pogue, Hill Roberts, Al Stewart, Russ Still, Howard Hong, Robert Heisterberg, Bruce Bickley, and Sharon Hart and my friends at The Balancing Program.

And finally, I would like to thank the many friends and relatives who have been a part of my life and my journey—I cannot possibly list them all, and the lovers and seekers of wisdom, and the teachers, too numerous to mention, whom I've encountered along the path.

About The Author

Ron Savarese studied journalism at Kent State University. He lives in Atlanta with his wife and their two dogs. They have two sons. This is his first novel.

Visit Ron at www.findtheopening.com

Book Clubs

If you are a member of a book club, or would like to start a book club with a group reading and discussion of this book, reading and study guides are available to help the group gain a deeper understanding of the subject matter. You can also arrange with Ron to make an interactive audio or video-call appearance to your group to speak and answer questions.